The Sting of Señorita Scorpion

A WESTERN TRIO

**Center Point
Large Print**

ॐ श्री गणेशाय नमः

LES SAVAGE, JR.

The Sting of Señorita Scorpion

A WESTERN TRIO

CENTER POINT PUBLISHING
THORNDIKE, MAINE

The text of this Large Print edition is unabridged.
In other aspects, this book may vary from the original
edition. Printed in Thailand. Set in 16-point
Times New Roman type by Bill Coskrey.

ISBN 1-58547-177-1

Library of Congress Cataloging-in-Publication Data

LC Control Number: 2001052962

TABLE OF CONTENTS

39/19   6-29-05

THE HANGMAN'S *SEGUNDO*

Les Savage, Jr.'s title for the story that follows was originally "Six-Gun Labarge." He completed it near the end of 1944 and sent it to the August Lenniger Literary Agency where he had been a client since August, 1943. His agent sent the story to Malcolm Reiss, general manager and editor of the Fiction House pulp magazines. Savage's *Señorita* Scorpion stories had been running with great success in *Action Stories* since early 1944. Reiss bought this story in early February, 1945, paying $300.00 for it. The author was only twenty-three years of age at the time. His extraordinarily wide reading and his mastery of historical details, for one so young, remain impressive. Under the title "The Hangman's *Segundo*" the story appeared in *Action Stories* in the issue dated Summer, 1945. For its first appearance ever in book form the text has been restored, according to the author's typescript, but the title used by the magazine has been retained.

I

IN the mirror above the bar, Kenny Kennison saw the two men rise from a table across the room behind him and move through the crowd his way, and he wondered if this was it, starting already. The first man had a smooth-skinned face that belied his close-cropped gray hair; it might have meant he was a younger man, turned prematurely gray, or an older man who hadn't worried much. If it meant he was older, it also meant he was dangerous, because a man in his profession who lasted long enough to turn gray naturally was either outrageously lucky or singularly deadly, and Saratoga Simms had never been famed for his luck.

Lean and slat-limbed in his square-cut ducking jacket and faded blue Levi's, Saratoga bellied up to the bar beside Kennison and spread his hands out, palms down. Kennison put his own hands on the bar, and there was something quietly potent in the long, slim fingers spreading pale against the dark mahogany. Kennison was still looking straight ahead into the mirror over the bar.

"Did it ever strike you, Saratoga, how much alike our hands are?" he said.

Saratoga was looking straight ahead, too. "A man's business marks him, Kenny. You here on business?"

Kennison's glance met his in the mirror. They both stood about the same height, but Kennison's shoulders held more breadth beneath the expensive cut of a dark blue steel-pen, so tailored that it showed no evidence of the shoulder harness he wore. There was a cool, impersonal, searching quality about his gray eyes, gleaming a little in the shadow cast by a black soft-brim, and his mouth crossed his clean-shaven chin in a hard, immobile line. He held up two fingers to the barman.

"Rye," he said softly.

The second man stood on Kennison's other side now, and he reeked of peach brandy, and Kennison knew that from here on out he would always associate the odor with the man, and he didn't particularly like the smell.

"Are you the gent Judge Barber brought in to guard his daughter?" he asked Kennison thickly.

7

"Acquaintance of yours, Saratoga?" asked Kennison.

"Name of Endee Labarge," said Saratoga.

"Oh," said Kennison, and glanced at the man in the mirror and saw that Endee Labarge was heavy about the shoulders, and that he had pulled his string tie loose to free a sweaty choke collar from a thick red neck. The blue growth of beard on his unshaven jaw covered a florid skin, and his bloodshot eyes wouldn't meet Kennison's. *They must be slipping*, thought Kennison, *if this is the kind they pick to do their jobs*.

"I asked if you were the man Judge Barber hired to guard his girl," said Endee Labarge again.

The barkeep shoved over a bottle, and Kennison poured his own drink before speaking. "What was the name?"

"Barber," said Saratoga. "Judge Barber."

Endee Labarge kept hitching self-consciously at the crossed cartridge belts of his two silver-mounted Colts. Kennison realized that up to now they had all been looking at each other only in the mirror. He wondered if maybe it would come when one or the other of them faced him directly. He held the rye up to the light, twirling the glass slowly.

"Oh," he said. "Judge Barber."

"Skip it," said Saratoga. "We know why you're here, Kenny. You don't want this job guarding the judge's daughter. It's a messy business. You always liked yours neat and clean. Did you come on the afternoon stage? It hasn't left yet . . .why not be on it when it leaves? How about New Orleans? Yeah, that was always a good town. You were there when I knew you last, Kenny, remember? Is that where you came from for this job? Why not go back? On the afternoon stage."

Kennison sniffed his drink deliberately, his face carefully inscrutable. This was the beginning of it, then. All right. It was his business, wasn't it? Sure. A hundred a week and keep. That's what they were paying him for the job. And if they wanted to begin it here, all right. "I'm tired of New Orleans," he said aloud, downed his rye unhurriedly, and rolled his tongue around in his mouth, testing it.

Saratoga spread his strong slender hands out a little more on the bar, studying them a moment. The batwing doors were shoved open, and a big, bearded man in faded Levi's came in, and the doors flapped back and forth a couple of times behind him, and stopped.

"I see," said Saratoga finally. "I see."

The reek of peach brandy swept Kennison anew as Endee Labarge's weight edged against him from that side. Kennison realized their intent. Either way he turned, there would be one of them behind him. All right. Moving with that unhurried deliberation, he reached for the bottle of rye and put the top back on. All right.

"Better change your mind," said Endee Labarge.

"Skip it," said Saratoga, looking up at the mirror again. "Kennison usually means what he says. He's tired of New Orleans. OK. So he's tired of New Orleans."

Go ahead, start talking, thought Kennison. *Start talking, Saratoga.* It was the way Saratoga worked. He was smooth. He covered his play with that lazy voice.

"I'm sorry you don't see it in a different light," began Saratoga, and he was watching Kennison intently in the mirror now. "A couple of pleasant gents have already been killed on this job, Kenny. I hate to see you stick your chin out. . . ."

Kennison had seen more than one man die with Saratoga talking like that, so lazily, so disarmingly. Endee Labarge kept shoving in against Kennison.

Kennison's voice was hardly audible. "Quit moving," he said.

"Yeah," said Saratoga, and his voice was softer, too. "Quit shoving, Endee. We're all gentlemen here. We'll do our business like gentlemen, won't we, Kennison . . . ?"

He took his hands off the bar as he said it and turned to look at Kennison squarely for the first time, and stepped back as he drove for his gun. As fast as Kennison moved, there was something deliberate and calculated about the way he clubbed the bottle, lunging forward with all his weight on the blow.

The bottle broke across Saratoga's wrist. Saratoga's .45 went off at the floor, and he dropped it with a sharp scream of pain. Not losing a motion, Kennison let go of the broken bottle and spun around. Labarge had shoved himself clumsily away from the bar. Kennison wasn't surprised to see that he hadn't gotten his fancy Colts out yet. He wasn't surprised to see Labarge stop them, half drawn.

"All right," said Kennison. "Go ahead. I'm waiting."

His voice was hardly more than a whisper, but its cutting edge carried to the farthest corner of the barroom in the sudden silence that had fallen. He stood with both hands held a little in front of him, empty. Endee Labarge gripped his Colts another moment, bloodshot eyes drawn in a fascinated way to Kennison's hands. The florid color drained from Labarge's cheeks. He lifted his hands off his guns with a sudden, jerky movement.

Saratoga stood, holding his bloody wrist, his face twisted like a whipped man. Kennison turned his back on them both and put his elbows carefully on the bar, holding up two fingers to the stunned barkeep.

"Rye," he said softly.

MARSHAL PHILIP GLENCOE came after Saratoga and Labarge had left. He was in his fifties, Glencoe, with level blue eyes and a clipped white mustache that matched the neat precision of his black frock coat and cream-colored Stetson. He introduced himself, read Kennison's letter of recommendation from Marshal Field in New Orleans.

"Field's a cousin of mine," said Glencoe. "He's written me about the work you did for him down there. Judge Barber wanted me to do the job, but I can't take any outside commitments like that. I suppose you'd like to know about it."

"You might say my interest has been whetted already."

"Good," said Glencoe, and nodded to the barkeep. "The usual, George! Well, Kennison, about fifteen years ago, when the mines around Point of Rocks here were going full blast, this was green pastures for bad men. The Jackson Hole Bunch was 'specially notorious. They worked for about five years, drove us nearly crazy. In all that time, we only found out who one of their number was. They pulled a job on Wells Fargo in Black Springs. There was a lot of shooting, and a Marshal Peterson was killed, along with the clerk in the office. Sixteen-year-old boy named Kid Hodge did the killing, and was wounded, and left behind by the gang. Judge Barber was practicing law in Black Springs at that time, and was in the Wells Fargo office when the hold-up occurred. He was the only witness to the shooting, and, while he couldn't identify the other members of the gang, his testimony sent Kid Hodge up for the murder of Marshal Peterson. When the sentence was passed, Kid Hodge stood up in the box and swore he'd come back and kill Barber and all his kin and the Jackson Hole Bunch to boot."

They finished their drinks and moved through the tables to the doors, and Kennison asked: "This is Kid Hodge, then?"

"After the judge and his daughter?" said Glencoe. "Yeah. At least Judge Barber thinks so. Kid Hodge broke jail some twelve years ago, three years after he'd been sent up, and the judge has been waiting for him to come back ever since. Sort of an obsession. Well, some three months back, the first attempt was made on Viola Barber's life. Since then, a Barber rider and a hired gunman have been killed while guarding her."

"Have you seen Kid Hodge?" asked Kennison.

"Fifteen years changes a person," said Glencoe. "Especially when he grows from a kid into a man. Since this business started, I've had every man in Point of Rocks pegged as Kid Hodge. Guess I'm just jumpy. It's a crazy business."

They worked through the milling, muttering crowd of men outside the Bitter Creek Saloon to where a newly painted buckboard stood at the curb. The driver was slouched over in his spring seat, one rundown boot heel jammed against the brake lever to hold the rig on the steep slant of the muddy street. Glencoe introduced him as Dallas Fenton. His shabby buffalo coat was pulled up around a sharp chin, his battered felt hat yanked down over his thin head, until most of his face was hidden. Kennison caught a momentary impression of bitter eyes as the man turned toward him, asking in a harsh, sullen voice: "Any bags?"

Kennison was trying to place him. "Left them at the stage dépôt."

Dallas Fenton kept his boot against the lever as he worked his matched bays out of the shifting crowd, and the dragging brakes shrieked all the way downhill, past the crazy cluster of miners' shacks and false-fronted buildings that formed the twisting street. In front of every doorway there were the crowds of men, their angry muttering hanging through Point of Rocks like the buzz of bees.

"What's the uproar?" Kennison asked.

"Has to do with your job, in a way," said Glencoe. "These men are from the Thayne Mines, which were closed down last week when I arrested their president. Besides Kid Hodge, Mason Thayne is the only one of the Jackson Hole Bunch we've ever seen. Along with the gold shipment which the Bunch got in that Wells Fargo hold-up, there were twenty thousand dollars worth of negotiable securities being shipped from here by the Farris Mining Corporation to its stockholders back East. We got the serial numbers on those securities, but they didn't show up till last month. The Thayne Mines have been pinching out this last year. They were approaching bankruptcy. I guess Mason Thayne had saved those Farris securities for just such a rainy day, and figured we wouldn't be looking for them, after fifteen years. But a marshal down in Abilene nabbed a fence who was handling the stuff, checked the serial numbers, traced them back to Thayne."

Kennison glanced at Glencoe, realizing suddenly that there was more than neat precision to the square cut of the marshal's face. It would take an infinite stubborn patience to keep plugging away at a case that long.

Then Fenton got off to get Kennison's bags at the dépôt, and Kennison caught the limp in the man's right foot and suddenly knew why Dallas Fenton had stirred a memory in him. It was an effort to keep the recognition from showing in his face. He had to force himself to speak calmly.

"Think Thayne will lead you to the rest of the Bunch?"

Glencoe shook his head. "Thayne himself won't talk. But the fence in Abilene claims there was a second party handling the Farris bonds jointly with Thayne. Evidently this second man and Thayne took the securities, which were worth more than the gold obtained in the hold-up but were more dangerous to handle, while the rest of the Bunch split up the bullion. The fence from Abilene wants leniency for turning state's evidence and won't identify this second member until we promise it to him. But the judge is the only one with the authority to cut anything off his sentence, and we'll have to wait till the trial to find out who the other man in with Thayne is. Maybe he'll talk more than Thayne did. Maybe that'll lead us to the rest of the Jackson Hole Bunch."

Fenton, climbing back into the buckboard, glanced at Glencoe, and Kennison caught the bitter intensity in those eyes again. Then the man had the reins and urged his horses into a trot that carried them out of town to the bottom of the steep hill and onto the road. Kennison felt a sudden chill as they passed into the cold, blue shadows cast by weird, potholed, gray cliffs, towering on either side. "Do you have any idea," he began, "who this second man . . . ?"

The shot crashed from above them, cutting him off. The high whine of lead and the screaming of the horses and Glencoe's shout were all intermingled.

"Jump for it," shouted the marshal. "They're on the cliffs!"

The team bolted to one side, the nigh horse rearing into the air and dragging the buckboard around in a vicious whipping half circle. Dallas Fenton jumped free from one side. Glencoe rolled off the other. But Kennison had been between them on the seat, and, before he could follow the marshal, the wagon crashed into the ditch and turned over. Kennison was thrown into the air with the thunder of another shot echoing from above.

For a moment he lay where he had landed in the chokecherry bushes, head rocking, earth soft and fetid in his face, coattails caught on the thorns above his head. Finally he shook himself and turned over on his belly. When he put his hands beneath him to rise, a shooting pain crippled his left wrist. He got to one knee, holding the sprained arm up against his chest.

The horses were still kicking and squealing, fighting to get free of the upset buckboard. Glencoe was lying on his belly in the ditch, ponderous .44 flaming at the cliffs across the road. He must have seen Kennison get his gun out and rise.

"Don't do it!" shouted Glencoe. "They've got a high-powered gun up there . . . !"

But Kennison was already dodging down the ditch in the

direction of town. The man above had fired three times now, with a distinct pause between each shot. It was what Kennison counted on. The rifle cracked, and dirt spewed up behind, tailing him.

He jumped out of the ditch, zigzagging across the road. A man handling a repeater could have raked him before he had taken two steps from the ditch. Kennison was almost across the road before the rifle blared again. Lead rattled through the chokecherry bushes banding the road in front of Kennison, now leading him.

He threw himself into the ditch on that side, knowing he had figured right. The rifleman was using a single-shot.

Taking advantage of that next interval in which the man would have to load again, Kennison cut through the scrub timber growing up the steep slope, then reached the cliff, the potholes giving it the appearance of a moldy dead face from which a thousand empty eye sockets stared into nothingness.

He worked upward, realizing how high the cliffs really were only when he turned to see Dallas Fenton and Marshal Glencoe, trying vainly to shelter themselves in the stunted timber below, minute, doll-like figures, pitifully exposed to whoever was on the clay above them. Already Fenton was hit. He lay holding his arm, huddled up in the bushes of the ditch.

Traveling laterally upward, Kennison reached a bench from which a narrow cut led back through the cliff. He saw other similar benches above. Then he caught movement on one of them. The rifle sounded louder now. Damp clay kicked into his face. He crouched in a pothole, curling his pale fingers around the bird's-eye butt of his gun.

In the catalog, it was an Iver Johnson .38 top-break five-shot, and it was shorter and lighter than most professionals cared for, and it took a good man to match such a gun against the ponderous two-and-a-half-pound Colts used by men like Saratoga. But Kennison had known what he was choosing, wanting a gun convenient for his shoulder harness and one with better balance, and he had yet to meet a Colt he hadn't been able to match.

Kennison had given the rifleman time to load. He set himself and rose from the pothole, dropping back. The rifle thundered. The slug took his hat off. Then he stood up again and crawled into the open unhurriedly.

Kennison climbed on up, waiting for the other man to load. Then he saw an upraised shoulder as the man tried to bring his rifle to bear. Kennison sent a deliberate shot at the pothole fifty yards above him. Clay kicked up on its lip, and the man dropped back into cover without firing. Kennison moved on up. The rifleman tried to fire again, and had to expose that shoulder and part of his face. Kennison squeezed the trigger on his second shot, forcing the man back down. Kennison moved on up.

There was something disparate about the way the man lurched into view for the third time. The Iver Johnson's bark was as cold and decisive as Kennison's advance. The rifleman cried out, and his rifle went off into the air, and he dropped back into the hole.

Still moving up, Kennison broke his revolver and swung the cylinder to the right, ejecting three empties with the automatic rod, getting three fresh loads from the pocket on his harness. He didn't get to use them.

When he reached the pothole, the only thing there was a

thick shred of acrid gunsmoke, the likes of which Kennison had never smelled before. There was a little pile of black powder, too, beside the imprints of a man's knee in the bottom of the depression. The pothole itself led into a gully that cut back through the cliffs. Droppings in the gully showed where the man had hitched his horse. Kennison looked back at the little pile of powder in the hole. It might have meant the man had spilled the powder from a horn. Kennison couldn't figure Saratoga Simms using an antiquated weapon like that.

When Kennison got back to the road, he helped Glencoe upright the light buckboard, uncoupling the tongue to use as a lever, and quieting the frenzied horse. Fenton stood to one side, holding his wounded arm, watching Kennison with a new speculation beneath the bitterness in his eyes.

"That's a sample of what you'll be bucking all the way in," said Glencoe. "Still think you want the job?"

"Back in New Orleans," said Kennison, "the Creoles serve *hors d'œuvres* before their main course."

"What," squinted Glencoe, "are they?"

"Appetizers," said Kennison.

II

JUDGE BARBER had built his house in the desolate country north from Point of Rocks, where the eroded, potholed cliffs had turned from their dead gray to a garish red, where predatory hawks hung on silent wings above the empty expanses of woolly Eaton sage. The wagon road passed a cluster of log cabins and several heavy pack-pole corrals and entered a steep-walled cañon that narrowed as it progressed, cliffs hanging over its dark bottom forbiddingly. It was the only approach to the house standing at its box end, a big frame structure, second story windows showing with closed shutters above the spread of green willows surrounding it. Fenton turned the buckboard around when Glencoe and Kennison had alighted, rattling back toward the cabins where he said his wife would fix his wound.

A Negro butler opened the massive oaken door, bowing low in his black cutaway and white waistcoat. He had a hollow voice, and the whites of his eyes gleamed as he rolled them at Kennison.

"The jedge is waitin' for you in the sittin' room," he said.

Kennison realized his fists were closed tight. He opened them, trying to relax and throw off the nervous tension that had been holding him ever since he left Point of Rocks. But this house only added to the strange eeriness of the whole business, standing silent and lonely back here, with only one way in or out, its windows shuttered and secret. From the small reception room another door opened into a narrow, wainscoted hallway that echoed sibilantly to the rustle of the butler's tail coat as he led them to the closed door at the other end. He knocked discreetly on the hand-carved portal, bound heavily with iron. Kennison heard the rattle of a key in the old-fashioned lock, and the door swung open on oiled hinges that made no sound.

His first impression was of a wall lined top to bottom with books, and then a fire blazing red in the stone fireplace, silhouetting the figure of a man standing with his back to the flames, his coattails lifted to warm his ample posterior.

The years had changed Judge Nathan Barber. His snow-white mane accentuated the florid red of his fat-jowled face, which might have come from high-blood pressure, or too many whisky and sodas, or both. He was bloated enough with rich living, but somehow he didn't take the stance a heavy man ordinarily assumed. Instead of throwing out his paunch with the usual, spread-legged ostentation, he stood so that there was almost a cringe in the way his shoulders seemed to shrink in on his neck as he bent forward, peering at Kennison with big, bloodshot eyes that popped from heavy lids like a frog's. Kennison was waiting rigidly for some sign of recognition in those eyes. He saw none.

"*Umph*," grunted Judge Barber, but his bluster wasn't convincing. "Very good, Mister Kennison? Yes, very good. Come in, please. And shut the door, Viola. How many times must I tell you?"

Perhaps some would have taken it for the natural irascibility of an old man. Kennison didn't. He had seen other men try to hide fear.

"I'll have to go back to town," said Glencoe. "I'm sure you'll be satisfied with Mister Kennison, Judge. He's already given me a few pointers this afternoon. I'll see you soon."

The girl who closed the door behind the marshal had raven hair that hung in a long silky bob over the collar of her white shirt. She wore high-heeled Western boots over English jodhpurs that were tailored more like the Mexican *charro* trousers Kennison had seen in Texas, lacking the usual flare above the knee and fitting tightly to the curve of her buttocks and legs, giving her figure a long, slim look.

He enjoyed it until he saw the angry pout of her rich lower lip, and realized it was for him.

"You'll have to excuse my daughter," said Judge Barber, clearing his throat. "She is against this business of having a . . . ah . . . guard, you might say. Yes, bodyguard."

"I'm not a child," said Viola Barber sharply.

"You are acting like one, my dear," said the judge. "Gallivanting around the country like a. . . ."

"I can't stay in the house all the time!" Her cheeks were flushed. "If I hid in here like you do, I'd be an old maid before they ever found this . . . this Kid Hodge. You've lived all your life in fear of his coming back, and now, when he does, you aren't even sure it *is* him!"

The judge choked when he tried to speak. He drew an asthmatic breath, and a little vein began to pound in his purpling neck. "You know it's him. If you'd only seen him there in the courtroom, standing up and swearing he'd come back to kill me and all my kin and every one of the Jackson Holers. Not an ordinary kid. Not shouting or ranting or making any hullabaloo. Almost whispering. And his eyes, Viola, his eyes. . . ."

"Maybe he had a bigger reason for doing it than just the fact that it was your testimony which convicted him," said Kennison.

Judge Barber's white head jerked around, and he took a step back and almost went into the fire. All the florid color had left his face; it was sallow and puffy and revolting, somehow. He tried to speak, and choked, and began to cough violently. He bent forward and had to grab the arm of a leather chair, still coughing. Viola ran to him, helping him down. She poured a drink from a cut-glass decanter, staring angrily at Kennison.

"You've upset him. Why did you say that?"

Judge Barber spilled the liquor on his white silk waist-coat when he drank it. Still sputtering and choking, he put the glass down and leaned forward, eyes popping at Kennison that way, his breathing hoarse.

"What do you mean . . . a bigger reason?" he said.

Kennison shrugged. "Seems to me it would take more than the mere fact that your testimony convicted him to make the kid that mad."

Barber's eyes had narrowed, and he shook his head, still watching Kennison. "Nothing else. I don't know what you mean. There wasn't anything more."

The Negro called again from outside the door, and Fenton came limping in when Viola unlocked it, holding his shoulder.

"Carterwright's here again," he said.

"Oh, Dad, that crazy fool," said Viola. "Why do you have anything to do with him? I'm going to tell him. . . ."

"You will tell him nothing," shouted her father, trying to rise. He fell back into the armchair, waving his hand vaguely at Fenton. "Let him in, let him in. And, Viola, please show Mister Kennison his room. You brought your clothes, Mister Kennison? Good. We'll dress for dinner."

The girl turned to the Negro. "Jeb. . . ."

"I asked you to show Mister Kennison his room, my dear," said Judge Barber.

Viola glanced at Kennison with a frown, shrugged slim shoulders. There was a stairway on either side of the great room, leading to balconies above, and Kennison realized that all the rooms in the house on both floors could be reached only from this parlor. Jeb brought Kennison's bags in. Kennison took them and followed the girl up the right hand stairway, finding it impossible to take his eyes from her tightly sheathed body. While he was still on the balcony, Fenton came into the lower room with another man. But the corner of the hall cut off Kennison from seeing who it was.

The hall led from the railed balcony to a door at its end, with other doors on either side. The girl opened the last one on the right into a large room with shuttered windows on either side of a huge four-poster. She lit the oil lamp on a round table beside the bed, its marble top covered with a green satin cloth. Kennison set down his bags and opened a suitcase and began to spread out his evening clothes, moving in his deliberate, unhurried way. He became aware that the girl had stopped in the doorway and was studying him. The cool appraisal in her big dark eyes disturbed him.

"What did you mean by that downstairs?" she said.

"I just wondered why the kid should get so hot under the collar," replied Kennison.

"No." She shook her head. "You meant something more. Who are you, Mister Kennison?"

"The man from New Orleans your father hired to guard you."

"And when you leave here, we won't know any more about you than when you came," she said. "You're that kind, aren't you?"

He unfolded his black swallow-tail and laid it on the bed. "You didn't seem that interested downstairs."

Her voice held a sudden anger. "My only interest is a dislike in being watched and hounded and tagged around everywhere I go by a . . . a gunman."

"There is a delicate distinction which you seem to have missed," he said. "A gunman, shall we say, is one who plies his trade extra-legally, while a man who uses his talent on this side of the law is more often called a gunfighter."

Her lip twisted almost contemptuously. "What's the difference? You get paid for what you do with a gun."

He kept himself from answering deliberately, wishing she would go now, wishing, somehow, that the judge didn't have a daughter who was so beautiful. He hadn't come here for that.

Then somebody started shouting downstairs, and the girl turned, and he caught something flung back over her shoulder as she ran out the door.

"It's Carterwright," she said. "I told Dad. . . ."

The voice coming from below was a crazy, guttural roar, more animal than human. Kennison followed the girl out and down the hall to where the balcony overlooked the lower room.

"You know what they'd do if I told them," bellowed the man from down there. "You know what'd happen to you. Give it to me now, Barber. I'm tired of waiting. Give it to me now. . . ."

A huge disheveled man with a mop of matted black hair was bending the judge back over the mahogany table, both hairy hands on the old man's purple neck, shaking him back and forth. Barber clawed futilely at the thick wrists, one shoe beating a spasmodic tattoo against the floor.

"Let him go, Carterwright!" shouted Dallas Fenton, trying to tear the big man off. "Let go, Carterwright!"

In that moment, Kennison recognized the big man, and

he was held there on the balcony by his surprise. Carter-wright! What did Fenton mean, Carterwright? Then he realized that most of them would have changed their names now, anyway.

The big hairy man let go of Barber with one hand, swept his arm around, knocking Dallas Fenton away. The girl was halfway down the stairs by then, but Kennison had seen how long it would take to reach them that way, and, as Dallas Fenton crashed into the bookcases and fell to the floor beneath Carterwright's blow, Kennison lifted his leg over the balcony rail. He moved swiftly without seeming to hurry. He let himself down over the other side until he hung by the flooring that extended out a few inches and provided a grip. It was only a few feet to the living room floor. He dropped without much sound, and Carterwright didn't know he was there till a moment later.

"Give it to me now, damn you," shouted the giant, hitting the judge across the face with one hand and knocking his head against the table. "Give it to me now, or you won't have to worry about Kid Hodge killing your daughter. They'd take care of that if I told. . . ."

The huge man's voice cut off in a sharp roar of pain as Kennison caught his arm by the elbow and yanked it around behind his back in a vicious hammerlock. It straightened Carterwright for that instant, forcing him to release the judge.

"Let him go, Kennison!" yelled Fenton, scrambling from the pile of books that had spilled over him when he crashed into the cases. "Leave him alone, Kennison!"

Carterwright spun around, his other arm flailing wildly. Kennison let go of the hammerlock. He ducked the arm.

He kicked Carterwright in the knee.

The big man couldn't help jerking spasmodically forward with a howl. Kennison caught his arm and pulled him on ahead and stuck a leg in front of his stumbling feet. Carterwright tripped over the leg. As he went down, Kennison hit him across the back of the neck. It was a wicked, calculated blow. Carterwright shook the floor and lay there without moving.

The whole thing had happened in an instant, and Kennison wasn't aware of his own draw after that. He only knew that he had seen Dallas Fenton getting up and going for his gun from the corner of an eye, and Kennison's own reaction was automatic. He stood there now, half turned around, facing the lame man.

Fenton sagged against the bookcase, grasping the shelf by which he had hauled himself erect with one hand, the other hand gripping the butt of a gun that wasn't yet free. His bitter eyes were on the Iver Johnson gleaming bluely in Kennison's pale hand, and there was a foolish look on his narrow, acrimonious face.

"Make up your mind, Mister Fenton," said Kennison. "Pull it out or shove it back in. I don't particularly care which."

III

THEY rode the next day, Kennison and the girl. She tried to slip out early without him, but the Negro butler had orders from the judge, and he woke Kennison and told him there was a horse already saddled out by the corrals. Now they were past the reddish cliffs and in the pasture land north of the judge's house, where Steamboat Valley spread its green grass to the dark hogbacks of the Vermilions farther on.

None of them had offered any explanation for Carterwright, but then Kennison in a way hadn't expected any, and he didn't especially need it. The only thing he didn't know about Carterwright was what business he had at the judge's house, and that didn't count much. Carterwright? Well, it was as good a name to take as any. As good as Dallas Fenton.

It had taken them a while to bring Carterwright around, after Kennison's blow. Kennison had expected the recognition in Carterwright's eyes, but he had expected some surprise, too, and there had been none, and that bothered him. He didn't give much thought to the hate he had seen in those eyes, along with the recognition. That would be taken care of when the time came.

"You did it so coldly," the girl said.

He looked up from his thoughts. "What?"

She was riding a fiddle-footed copper chestnut with a mane like yellow flax, running maybe fourteen hands tall beneath her silver-plated Cheyenne saddle. She had apparently resigned herself to Kennison's company and was watching him in a sidelong, studying way.

"How you hit Carterwright," she said. "I've never seen it done so coldly. You do everything that way, don't you? Coldly. Deliberately."

He shrugged. "Something I learned early in life. Use your head and you don't lose it. Only you can't use it to your best advantage when you're excited, can you?"

"So you never get excited," she said. "You don't allow

yourself to get mad, or laugh, or do anything without planning it all ahead. Do you enjoy being a machine?"

It was sarcastic, and he wanted to tell her a man lived longer if he did these things, but he kept his mouth closed on the words and his face inscrutable, watching the way her silky hair bobbed against her white shirt, and wishing again that she hadn't entered into this.

They were following a faint trail that led up over the top of ruddy buttes, looking down onto the main floor of the valley. He headed Viola's chestnut off the trail and through a cut so they wouldn't be skylighted, topping the rise, then halted at the mouth of the gully. The blue grass spread out like a soft carpet below them. A bunch of Barber steers browsed close to a stream that curled down from the yonder slope of the Vermilions.

"You seem to enjoy it," she told him.

He felt the caustic tone and couldn't help his abrupt answer. "Why not? High grass and fat cows and deep water. Any man would be proud to own a spread like this."

"I didn't know you were interested in cattle," she said.

"Maybe more than you think."

"Oh," she smiled. "Oh. You have plans. I'll bet you mapped it all out from the start. How like you. I'm not going to be a gunman all my life . . . I'll shoot five men a year and get five thousand dollars for every man I shoot, and in five years I'll have enough to buy myself a spread. . . ."

Kennison's mare shied at his hard jerk on the reins, breaking forward suddenly and sliding down through the talus. Behind, he could hear the girl laughing—at him.

"You're angry," she said almost triumphantly. "I didn't

think you had any feelings. I didn't think anything could touch you."

All right, he thought. *All right.* Sure he was angry. No other woman had ever made him feel angry; no other woman had made him feel much of anything. Why this one?

It was disturbing, though, how she had struck home. It was just the way he had looked at it, planning ahead and saving toward the day when he could quit and have such a spread. He shrugged his shoulders, a hard line coming to his mouth, and deliberately dismissed the anger.

There were some hands stringing new wire on the other side of the valley. Dallas Fenton sat on the spring seat of the Studebaker wagon in which they had hauled the bales. Kennison felt the man's eyes on him all the way across the meadow. A pair of riders broke away from the group to meet Viola as she halted her chestnut slightly ahead of Kennison.

One of them was Endee Labarge. His perpetually flushed face was clean-shaven now, and he wore a pair of batwing chaps that didn't make him look any more like a cowhand than his fancy guns made him look like a gunman. He edged his big dun up to the man riding with him, looking at Kennison.

"That's him, Dad," he said. "That's Kennison."

Dad? Colonel, then, thought Kennison, *Colonel Jack Labarge.* He hadn't changed as much as Judge Barber. He was bigger than his son, but where Endee Labarge's weight was all soft dissipation, Colonel Jack's was solid authority. The colonel's face was as ruddy as his son's, but the color came from the outdoors rather than peach brandy. His John

B. set squarely on a leonine mane of black hair, parted in the middle, and his black eyes weren't bloodshot, and they emanated a stubborn, adamantine strength, meeting Kennison's gaze for a long, silent moment.

"Kennison," he stated finally, and his voice was as heavy and authoritative as his seat in the saddle. "Kennison. Haven't I seen you somewhere before?"

"How are the mines?" asked Kennison.

Colonel Jack's double-rig squeaked as he thrust his weight forward in a surprised way. "Mines? They've been closed for five years, Mister Kennison. How would a man from New Orleans know about them?"

"New Orleans?" said Kennison. "Did Saratoga tell you I was from there?"

"Who?" asked Colonel Labarge.

"You got the name," said Kennison.

It might have been anger that turned Labarge's black eyes cloudy like that, but he controlled it well. He stared intently at Kennison, patiently trying to fathom that pale, quiet immobility. Then he straightened in his saddle, turning pointedly to Viola.

"I want to invite you and your dad over to dinner Saturday night, Viola. It's been a long time."

Viola smiled. "Thanks, Colonel Jack. It'll do Dad good to get out."

The genuine heartiness in Colonel Jack's laugh surprised Kennison. "You bring that old mossy horn over, if you have to hitch a pair of buggy mares to him."

Endee got his horse in between Kennison and the girl and edged her away, saying something. The girl laughed softly. The elder Labarge turned back to Kennison.

"I understand the judge has hired you to guard Viola. I suppose you'll be coming, too?"

"I suppose," said Kennison. "Will Saratoga be there?"

"Why do you keep referring to this . . . this Saratoga?" Kennison's voice was mocking. "Oh, now, Mister Labarge. . . ."

"*Colonel*," said Labarge. "Colonel Labarge. This Saratoga, now . . . ?"

Kennison was aware that Viola and Endee were drifting down toward the cottonwoods by the river. He turned to follow them as he spoke. "I don't think I have to tell you about Saratoga, do I, Mister Labarge? Or aren't you aware of the company your son is keeping?"

"Kennison," called Colonel Jack. "You let the girl and Endee alone."

"I wasn't referring to the girl," said Kennison, and turned his horse completely around.

Before he could gig it forward, Colonel Jack spurred his big black Morgan into a trot and cut around in front of Kennison and came back till his horse stood with its head by the rump of Kennison's mare, and its tail up by the mare's head. With the animals side by side like that, Labarge faced Kennison. He reached out a square hand with knuckles like chopped granite, grasping the lapel of Kennison's short coat.

"I think you are deliberately antagonizing me, Mister Kennison," he said. "I'm not used to that. I'll give you a chance to apologize."

Kennison was vaguely aware that the men had dropped the wire and were watching intently. Dallas Fenton bent forward on the Studebaker, sharp face pale, waiting. Kennison's controlled voice held the sibilant threat of a gun whispering from its leather.

"Take your hands off me, Mister Labarge."

For another moment Labarge stared into Kennison's cold gray eyes. Perhaps it was what he saw in them. His mouth opened slightly as if he were going to speak. He didn't speak. His big fist opened slowly, dropping away from the lapel.

Kennison gave his mare the boot and left in a dead silence. He was conscious of Colonel Jack's sitting the black Morgan there, watching him all the way down to the river, fist still held up in the air a little, a dull, dangerous red creeping into the heavy strength of his face.

Viola and Endee were standing by the river, watering their horses, and Kennison thought Endee was closer to Viola than he had to be.

"Did you have to tag along?" Endee asked Kennison angrily.

"You do your sparking some other day," said Kennison.

For a moment, Endee stood there quivering like a spooked broomtail, then he turned and jammed a raging boot into his stirrup without stopping to tighten his cinch. The saddle slipped over with his weight, and he had to hop around on one foot before he could tear his boot from the stirrup. Swearing, he heaved the rig back around and cinched up with a vicious jerk. He climbed on again and tore the horse's mouth, pulling violently on the reins to get it turned around.

Viola's face was flushed, and her eyes flamed at Kennison. Then she turned around to tighten her own cinch, and he saw her slim shoulders trembling. At first he thought she was crying. Then he realized she was laughing. His mouth twisted up at one side in a strange, crooked way. She caught it as she stepped aboard her chestnut. The laughter left her, and something softened in her eyes.

"You smile, too," she said, and it wasn't sarcastic this time.

"On rare occasions," he said.

She swung her animal around and cut through the grove of cottonwoods to a trail that paralleled the river up toward the Vermilions. He came up with her, and they rode silently for a long time before they spoke.

"I'm going to see Carterwright," she told Kennison. "He's been squatting on our land in the Vermilions, and Dad won't do anything to get him off."

"I thought ranchers were death on squatters," he said.

"We don't have any pastures in the mountains," she said. "An ordinary squatter on this part of our spread wouldn't bother us. But Carterwright's been causing trouble. I don't think he's right in the head. There's been some small-time rustling, too, that no big operators would touch. You saw that cut in the fence. That's where the last bunch was run through."

"And the judge won't do anything about it?"

"Carterwright's got some sort of hold over Dad," she said. "I never was able to find out what. I'm tired of it. I'm going to tell Carterwright he'll have to get off our land, or I'll have the marshal out here."

It was rugged, wild country, high in the Vermilions, country that Kennison thought no one knew about—at least no one like Viola. As they rose through the somber stands of lodge-pole pines, with dead cones crackling

33

beneath the horses' hoofs and startling the empty silence, Kennison began to see that the girl was following a definite route, and it began to come back to him.

Late in the afternoon they turned down the narrow valley that ended at a wall of solid granite, rising harsh and implacable, to block their way.

"You can get a horse up there if you want to take the time," said the girl. "It would be easier to hitch down here."

Only one who knew the trail could have found it, up the sheer cliff, a series of branches and cuts, some made by nature and erosion, others looking as if they had been hacked out by man. Kennison saw scars all along the way that might have been made by shod hoofs, some fresh, some old and dim. It was a long, hard, sweating climb, but finally they stood on the lip of the wall. For it was a wall, literally, and on its other side the narrow cañon continued, spreading out into a round, bowl-like valley heavy with timber. The sides of the cañon rose on above the girl and the man to steep higher slopes, so that not even an experienced mountaineer would have guessed the existence of this part of the cañon unless he were directly above it.

They moved precariously down the other side, dropping from rock to rock. They came to a place where the trail forked around a big boulder. The girl took the left branch, stepping out onto the narrow bench. Kennison jumped after her.

"Viola! Not that way."

His hand caught her arm as the shale gave way beneath her feet. One of her boots slipped off with the crumbling rock. For that moment her weight fell outward, pulling Kennison with it. Desperately he heaved himself backward, holding onto her. They stumbled back against the boulder and fell there, breathing heavily. The girl's fascinated eyes were on the sandstone, dripping off the trail into the emptiness below. She turned to Kennison.

"How did you know," she almost whispered. "Nobody could have seen that rotten stone. Have you been here before?"

He didn't answer. He helped her up and took the right fork of the trail and led on down. They cut into a bunch of canoe birch and moved through the white gleaming trunks to a clearing. A clay-banked spring gurgled up from a clump of bushes weighted heavily with dark red serviceberries that only an Indian could swallow and not grimace. Above the spring was the cabin, ancient logs not dressed down, earth banked up for the foundation. The split-railed corral behind was empty, but an old Nelson double-rigged saddle hung on the top bar. From somewhere a meat bird cackled. It was the only sound.

"A man could live here a long time without being found," said Kennison, almost to himself. "Anybody else know about it besides you?"

She shook her head. "Nobody ever rides this part of our spread. And who could find it by themselves? I trailed Carterwright one day. I couldn't have followed him by his tracks. He backtracked and double-trailed and followed the river. But I kept him in sight and made a couple of good guesses, when I lost him once, and managed to hang on till he got here. Then I saw him drag his horse up that cañon wall."

"It looks like we've come while he's away visiting," said Kennison. "You stay here while I have a look around."

He moved into the open cautiously, watching the shadowed timber across the way for any movement. The door
hung on rawhide hinges, and there was no lock. Nothing
much had changed. The bunks were still tiered around the
back room, one of them containing a fetid roll of blankets.
A plank table stood on rickety legs of split pine, rusty tin
cans scattered around beneath it, the boards greasy and
covered with tallow from several candles. He found a
sougan by the fireplace, emptied out a checked shirt and a
pair of Levi's, both for an unusually large man. Then from
outside Viola called.

"Kennison. Look out. Kennison . . . !"

He had his gun from its shoulder harness before he was
clear of the cabin. The first thing he saw was the girl, running from the timber into the clearing. Whatever she was
looking at was blocked off from his sight by the corner of
the cabin. He would also be out of sight to whoever was
back there. But the girl wouldn't.

Kennison was still running toward her. He twisted
around, when Carterwright charged around the end of the
shack. The big man was looking at Viola, and he held a
rifle across his belly.

"Viola!" he shouted. "Damn you!" He brought up the
gun.

Kennison saw his intent, and fired. Carterwright's face
contorted suddenly, and it might have been from the pain,
or just the surprise of seeing Kennison for the first time.
Then the big man stumbled and tried to get his rifle up.
Kennison fired again. Carterwright's rifle bellowed from
the ground as he fell.

Spooked by gunfire, a horse whinnied up by the corral

and ran a few feet, and then stopped, held down by the trunk of the tree Carterwright must have been dragging in for his firewood. The dally was drawn taut from the saddle horn to the log, and the horse kept jerking on it. Kennison had reached Carterwright by then and hunkered down beside him, and saw how it was. The rifle was an ancient Sharp's muzzleloader. Kennison remembered that little pile of black powder back in the pothole of the cliff near Point of Rocks.

Carterwright opened his eyes, and that crazy, dull look was gone from them now. He saw Kennison looking at the rifle, and nodded weakly. "Yeah," he mumbled. "That was me on the cliffs back by town. I was in the Bitter Creek Saloon when you had that tiff with Saratoga. I recognized you. Maybe the judge didn't recognize you, or Dallas Fenton. But I couldn't miss my own kin."

"But why that business on the cliffs?"

"Why?" asked Carterwright, surprised. "Why not? I just thought I'd get you before you got me, that's all. It didn't matter that I'd changed my name. I knew you'd recognize me as soon as you got a look. You couldn't miss your own kin. Just like I knew you. You know me. I don't blame you. You had every right."

"No," said Kennison harshly. "No. I didn't come back after you. If you hadn't tried to shoot the girl. . . ."

"I didn't know you were here," mumbled Carterwright. "I saw Viola coming out of the timber and yelling, and I thought she'd brought the whole pack down on me. I didn't see you until too late. I'm not in with the others, though. This was my own loop. The judge'll tell you that. I'm not doing this with the others. . . ."

Kennison saw it was coming, and grabbed Carterwright. "Doing what? What others?"

"I don't blame you. You know me. . . ."

The lined, bearded face relaxed, and his heavy body relaxed, and Kennison let him drop back. He realized the girl was standing above them, watching his own face instead of the dead man's.

"You *do* know him," she said. "Who is he, Kennison? What did he mean by *the others?* Who is he?"

IV

COLONEL JACK LABARGE'S house was built across the Green River from where Jim Bridger had erected his fort in earlier years. It was a large, imposing structure on the granite bluffs above the river, with a steep hip roof over its verandah, which overlooked the turbulent waters below. Dallas Fenton had driven the buckboard, dressing in a frock suit for the occasion. Colonel Jack met them at the front door. He seemed to have forgotten what had occurred the other day, and Kennison didn't like that, somehow.

Labarge ushered them into the parlor where his son and another man stood. He was lean and slat-limbed, looking uncomfortable in a cutaway and broadcloth trousers, a man who had a smooth-skinned face that belied his close-cropped gray hair.

"Mister Kennison," said Colonel Jack, "will you meet . . . ?"

"We've met," said Kennison, "several times in the past." His eyes ran the length of Saratoga's coat. "It's not like you to come unequipped, Saratoga."

Saratoga smiled, unperturbed. "You here in an official capacity, Kenny?"

Viola was watching them narrowly. Kennison hadn't told her who Carterwright was. It would have meant telling her how he knew, and that would have finished all of it in a way he didn't want it finished right now.

They moved into the dining room where a long table was set with snowy linen and heavy Spanish silver service. Kennison sat next to Colonel Jack's wife, a small, vague woman who kept pulling nervously at her black pelisse. Patently she had been under Labarge's domination from their wedding night onward. After dinner, Viola and Mrs. Labarge left the gentlemen to their smokes. Kennison stood in the big doorway of the library, watching the two women go upstairs, his eyes thoughtful.

"Panatela, Kennison?"

Kennison declined the box of cigars Colonel Jack was holding out. He moved into the library, where the others were, a big room with French windows along its south wall. There were slatted shutters outside to protect the glass portals during the winter, but now they were thrown open. The judge had settled into the deep armchair in front of the huge fireplace formed from scores of round granite nigger-heads. Endee Labarge stood with an elbow on the rough-hewn mantel, watching Kennison sullenly. Colonel Jack bit off the end of his panatela, spat it into the fire.

"We were talking about Mason Thayne, Kennison," he said. "What do you think?"

"Why ask me," said Kennison, looking to where Saratoga stood in the library doorway now, a faint smile on his youngish face.

"You seem to know Point of Rocks better than any man from as far south as New Orleans really should," said the colonel, and didn't try to make his laugh pleasant. "About the Jackson Hole Bunch, for instance. I claim a man as big as Thayne wouldn't be fool enough to mess around with small-time hold-up artists like that. What do you say?"

"Maybe, when the Jackson Hole Bunch was operating, Mason Thayne wasn't as big as he is now," said Kennison.

The colonel chuckled. "Yeah. I thought that's about what you'd say. Madeira? Madeira, gentlemen?"

Kennison took the wine, held it up to the light, twirling the small glass slowly. His long fingers had that quietly potent look to them, pale against the dark liquid. Perhaps Dallas Fenton saw it. He stood with his back to the French windows, and his narrow eyes were on Kennison's hand, speculation in them.

"There's talk of a second party being mixed up with those securities Mason Thayne was supposed to have unloaded," said Colonel Jack, watching smoke curl from his cigar.

Judge Barber looked up from his chair. He gulped his drink, leaned over the side for another from the table, still watching Labarge. He poured himself the wine, blustering: "Just talk. *Hmmph.* Yes, just talk. If that fence knew who the second party was, why didn't he tell them when he identified Thayne?"

"According to Glencoe, the fence is using his knowledge of the other man to get some years sliced off his own sentence," said Fenton. "He won't talk till they promise him leniency."

"Excuse me," said Endee Labarge, and went past Kennison.

Barber's hand trembled when he raised the glass to his lips. The wine spilled onto his white waistcoat. The gleaming red drops reminded Kennison of blood. Then he wondered suddenly if he had eaten too much. He felt dizzy, looked around for Saratoga, and couldn't find him. *Where had the man stood?*

"Maybe the fence doesn't know who the second party is," said Barber, stumbling over his words. "He might be stalling."

"Might be," said Labarge, smoke rings rising from the small circle of his mouth. "If he were stalling, I don't think Glencoe would stand much chance of finding out who the rest of the Bunch were. Thayne wouldn't talk. He's tough. He wouldn't welsh on the rest of the gang, would he, Judge?"

"No," said the judge. He tried to rise, and failed. "No, Jack, he wouldn't talk. He's tough. Yeah."

"Have another drink, Judge," suggested Labarge. "You, Kennison? No? Imported stuff. As I recall it, Judge, those Jackson Holers were all pretty tough. If one of them was in line to welsh on the others, I imagine it would go pretty hard with him, wouldn't it?"

The judge drew a wheezing breath, eyes popping at Labarge. He took the drink Colonel Jack had poured, gulping it, wiping his mustache hastily. Kennison had to grab a chair to keep from falling. The room seemed to grow larger, then smaller. The walls rushed in at him and receded, changing hues.

"On the contrary," laughed Colonel Jack. "Have

another drink."

Kennison reached the double doors leading into the dining room. He hadn't remembered closing them. He tried to shove them apart and was startled at his own weakness. Then he realized it wasn't weakness. They were locked.

He turned around, feeling sick, and then more than sickness, a strange, sharp fear that wasn't for himself. Labarge's voice seemed to come from a distance.

"You look pale, man. Sit down. Have some wine."

Kennison lurched past him. Colonel Jack tried to grab his arm, and Kennison shook him off, reaching the French windows. Fenton was in his way somehow then, and Kennison noticed abstractedly that the man hadn't downed his drink.

"Better do like Colonel Jack says, Kennison."

Kennison jostled the glass so the wine spilled out when he pushed Fenton away. He grabbed the small gilt handles of the windows, trying to open them. They wouldn't work. He rattled the portals savagely.

"What are you doing?" called Labarge, jumping at him.

Dallas Fenton grabbed at his shoulder, and Colonel Jack caught his arm, trying to pull him away from the doors.

Kennison suddenly whirled. "Damn you," he slurred thickly, and tripped Dallas Fenton into Colonel Jack, and shoved them both hard against the judge's chair. They fell to the floor with a crash, and Kennison was already turned back to the French windows. Breathing heavily, he began to kick the glass out of the door. He smashed each pane out deliberately, taking the framework with it. The glass tinkled and crashed all over his leg, and then the higher panes shivered, and he lifted his boot to clean them out.

"Kennison!" he heard Labarge shout.

Kennison was bent over already, stepping through the space he had made. A sliver of glass caught at his coat. He jerked it off, heard the cloth rip. His last view of the men was a hazy, warped one through the broken pattern of glass still in the windows. Colonel Jack was trying to kick free of Fenton, holding one hand out toward Kennison, his mouth open. The judge was turned around in his seat, eyes popping weirdly. The stone verandah echoed to Kennison's stumbling boots as he half ran to the corner and around to front of the house, yanking open the front door. Mrs. Labarge was coming down the front stairs, hitching at her pelisse.

"Viola?" he asked, shaking his head groggily.

"Viola?" she said. "Oh, yes. She went out with Endee, I think. Yes, spring, you know. Young people, you know."

He turned back onto the verandah. *So they went outside,* he thought, and tried to keep thinking it because his mind was wandering, and he had to concentrate on something. *So they went outside. They locked the doors, and they went outside. . . .*

An owl was calling softly from the grove in front of the house, and the moonlight caught the yellow leaves of the poplars in a pale, shining pattern, and for a moment Kennison wondered if maybe he was mistaken, it seemed so peaceful. Then he caught the shadowy movement in the trees.

"What was that noise?" someone asked.

The answer was muffled, and Kennison recognized neither of the voices. "Maybe Kennison fell through a window. It's about time that stuff took effect. Come on. They're down by the railing."

Kennison moved without much sound, as sick as he was, and the heady resinous scent of the poplars closed around him. The owl hooted again. Voices came from ahead then, not the same ones as before.

"But you're of age now, and you can give me your answer, Viola. I don't want to wait. . . ."

"What decision, Endee?"

"I thought it was understood. . . ."

"Too much to understand, Endee. You've taken too much for granted always. I never gave you to understand anything."

The shadowy movement came between the voices and Kennison. He knew what he had to do now. His knees felt wobbly, and he wanted to lie down and be sick somewhere, and he couldn't see very well, but he knew what he had to do.

He moved a little closer. He could see Endee and the girl, standing by a rail on the edge of the bluff. The moonlight caught Endee's flushed face as he turned to look back over his shoulder, then spoke to Viola again.

"Let's not quarrel. You're all upset about this Kid Hodge business. Maybe when it's over. . . ."

There was another movement between them and Kennison. It was his time. He jumped forward and struck at the first shadowy bulk with a vicious downward swipe of his gun. The man fell away from Kennison without a sound, rolling into the open almost at Viola's feet. She turned with a sharp cry.

Endee caught her by the shoulders. "Saratoga?" he shouted.

Kennison hit at the second man, heard the sharp rip of his

gun barrel tearing cloth. The man cried out and lurched away. Kennison stumbled across the one he had knocked down and fell against the girl and Endee.

"Saratoga?" shouted Endee again, still trying to hold Viola.

Kennison had to grab at Endee to keep from going clear down, and he straightened, hearing someone running away through the poplars. "Is that who you expected?" he asked.

"Kennison!" gasped Endee Labarge.

Kennison only needed a glance at the man, lying on the ground. He saw the smooth face and the gray hair, and beyond that he didn't care. The answers would have to come later. All he knew now was that he had to get the girl home before he went out completely. He shook his head viciously, trying to clear it, and grabbed Viola by the arm.

She winced. "Let me go."

"You're coming with me," he said. "We're going home."

She looked into his face, and her dark eyes widened, and suddenly all the resistance left her. Kennison pulled her across the unconscious Saratoga. Endee tried to stop them.

"Look here, Kennison. . . ."

"Leave me alone, Endee," said Kennison.

Endee stopped with his hands still held out, and Kennison and the girl left him like that. Kennison guided Viola through the grove by an elbow. She went all the way without a word, looking up into his face as if she had found something in it she had never seen before. He reached the verandah and heard Judge Barber's wheezing voice coming from the library.

"I tell you, Jack, she's been gone too long. How do you know she's with your son? I'm going out to find her."

"Now, Judge," said Colonel Jack's deep voice. "You've been drinking a lot, and you're unduly upset. If something's happened to Viola. . . ."

"You anticipate, Mister Labarge," said Kennison, from the French window he had smashed open. "Nothing has happened to Viola. Nothing will. We're going home."

Judge Barber tried to rise from the leather armchair. "There you are, Kennison. We don't have to go yet. . . ."

"Get your coat on, Judge," said Kennison. "We're going home."

V

AT first Kennison thought it was someone hitting him on the head. Then he realized they were pounding on his door. He rolled over and put his legs to the floor, wincing as the judge's screaming beat on his brain from the hall outside.

"Open your door, Kennison! Viola's gone! Kid Hodge's got her! Open up!"

Kennison rose from the bed with an effort, unlocked his door. Judge Barber burst in, white hair disheveled above his purple face, eyes wild. Glencoe came in behind him, dusty and stoop-shouldered from the long ride.

"He's right, Kennison," snapped the marshal. "I just got here with Jeb. Viola's room is empty. Is that why you sent the Negro after me last night?"

For a moment, Kennison looked at them blankly, unable to believe it. "Of course not. I locked Viola in her room last night." He turned to Barber suddenly. "Who else has any keys?"

"Dallas Fenton," said Barber, then his mouth sagged, and he shook his head. "No, Kennison. No. You're mistaken. Dallas has been with me too long. It's Kid Hodge, I tell you. Kid Hodge!"

His voice had risen to a shrill crescendo, and he broke off, gasping, coughing. He stumbled to the bed, fighting for breath, sinking onto the quilt.

Kennison slipped on his pants with a swift deliberation. "You've been so obsessed with the idea of Kid Hodge coming back to kill you that you're blind to anything else," he told the judge. "I thought maybe I could save your daughter before they tried to get her again."

"What do you mean ... before *they* tried?" Barber almost screamed. "It's Kid Hodge ... !"

Kennison buckled on his shoulder harness, snuggled the Iver Johnson in. "I would have told you this sooner, Glencoe, but I didn't know until last night that it was the Jackson Hole Bunch trying to get Viola. And I didn't know Colonel Jack Labarge was one of the Bunch. You want the rest of them? There's one buried up in the Vermilions who went by the name of Carterwright ... he used to be Lee Curry. Dallas Fenton's real name is Oliver Warren. He got that limp in a hold-up about a year before the Wells Fargo job at Black Springs. Judge Barber didn't have to change his name. He stayed in the background, like Labarge."

The judge stiffened, turning slowly pale. His breath came out spasmodically, and he clutched at his heart. His pop-eyes were staring at Kennison.

Kennison put on his coat, voice unrelenting now. "I'm going after your daughter, Judge. You'd better not stall. The more time we waste here, the less chance she'll have."

47

Barber tried to speak, choked on his words, then shook his head resignedly. "You're right, Kennison. There isn't any use hiding things any longer. I won't last to see my daughter again, anyway, even if you can get her back. These last few months have finished my heart, and this morning was the final shock. My doctor warned me. All right, Glencoe. My lawyers in New York have an envelope that isn't to be opened until my death. It holds a confession of everything. I'm the man who was holding those securities with Thayne . . . that would have come out as soon as the fence from Abilene talked. About a year after that Wells Fargo job, the gang broke up. Saratoga Simms and Lee Curry drifted south. Dallas Fenton stayed with me. Lee Curry came back three years later under the name of Carterwright, practically insane from too much drinking. Hid out in the Vermilions somewhere. Threatening to expose me if I didn't keep him in money. When I was slow with payment, he rustled my stock. He was after money the day you arrived, Kennison."

Kennison's face was bleak. "Carterwright . . . or Lee Curry . . . was Kid Hodge's half-brother. Kid Hodge had a talent with a gun, and Lee Curry was always trying to get him in with the gang, even took him to their hide-out a couple of times. But Kid Hodge didn't want any of it. He was working in Black Springs the day of the robbery, and, when he saw the Bunch begin to drift in, he guessed what was up. Tried to warn the Wells Fargo people. He was still in the office when the Bunch hit. Marshal Peterson came running in from the back room. Lee Curry murdered him and the clerk, then knocked Kid Hodge unconscious, sticking a gun in his hand."

Judge Barber nodded dully. "I was in the office, purportedly on business, really to give the high sign to Curry when the coast was clear. As the only eyewitness, my testimony convicted Kid Hodge. We didn't want the government on our tail, and we thought, if they had a murderer for their marshal, they'd drop the case."

Glencoe whistled. "No wonder Kid Hodge swore he'd come back and get you."

"Yes," said Barber. "He had a bigger reason than just the fact that my testimony convicted him. He must have guessed I was hooked up with the Bunch somehow when I gave that false testimony. But he couldn't prove anything. He didn't know about Labarge, and he didn't even try to tell about his half-brother. Just got up there and swore he'd come back like that. And his eyes, Glencoe, if you'd only seen his eyes. . . ."

"But why try to get your daughter like this?" said Glencoe. "Why not just kill her, and you?"

"It isn't Kid Hodge," said Kennison. "Can't you understand that? The man who was handling those securities with Thayne was Judge Barber. As soon as the fence talked, you'd have nabbed the judge. Maybe Thayne wouldn't reveal who the rest of the Bunch was. But what about Barber? The man who was afraid? The man who had built his house on fear, who reared his daughter on it, who lived with it and in it all his life?"

"If they wanted to stop his mouth, why not just kill him?" snorted Glencoe.

"With his confession ready to be opened on his death?" said Kennison. "No. They had to shut him up another way. That's what they were trying last night, only the dope they

49

put in my drink didn't act as fast as they'd planned. They knew all the marshals in harness couldn't make the judge open his mouth if it meant his daughter would be harmed."

"But not Dallas," mumbled Barber. "He frustrated two attempts to get Viola before you came."

"Maybe he was loyal at first," said Kennison, "but he would be exposed along with the others, if you talked. Maybe it took them this long to persuade him. I don't know. All I know is I locked her in last night."

Barber was clutching his heart. "Kennison, I'm dying. If you're right, she won't be any use to them with me gone. They'll get rid of her. They'll kill me, and you don't even know where they've taken her. . . ."

"There was one place the Jackson Hole Bunch took about everything they got," said Kennison.

A delirious light came into Barber's pop-eyes, and he began to babble. "But if you're wrong. If it's Kid Hodge . . . ?"

Kennison grabbed him by the shoulders. "Kid Hodge never came back to get you or anybody else. He had time in jail to find out that wasn't the way."

"How do you know?" said Glencoe.

Kennison let go of the judge, straightening slowly. "Most of the Bunch changed their names when they broke up." He looked at Glencoe. "I changed mine. *I'm Kid Hodge.*"

VI

GRAY serpents of clammy ground fog writhed up the sheer escarpment of that narrow valley deep in the wild Vermilions. Night was falling, and Kennison and Glencoe had hitched their jaded horses among the other unguarded mounts at the bottom.

"You see how safe they think it is," said Kennison, climbing the first section of the trail. "Not even leaving a guard. I don't know who'll be here, Glencoe, but if you're the one to meet Saratoga, don't let him start talking."

Glencoe sweated behind him. "Smooth?"

"Like silk," said Kennison. "An old-timer. If you get the drop on him, make him unbuckle his hardware the first thing. If it's an even up, shovel your iron before he can open his mouth."

They were almost at the top, and Kennison was looking partly down when he saw the sudden surprise cross the marshal's face. Glencoe flattened against the rock, pawing at his .44, looking wide-eyed up past Kennison.

"Watch it!" he shouted. "Watch it . . . !"

Kennison threw himself flat against the granite as Glencoe's voice was drowned by the bellow of a gun. The marshal grunted with pain. Kennison had his gun out then, but it all happened before he could shoot, or even look up. Marshal Glencoe leaned away from the rock, blood spreading across his shirt front, his face stamped with the incredible effort of will it must have taken to raise his .44 and fire twice past Kennison. Then he dropped the ponderous six-gun and collapsed, beginning to fall from the rock.

A body hurled past Kennison from above. He caught the twisted, bitter face of Dallas Fenton.

Then Kennison had slid down to Glencoe, grabbing him beneath the armpits. He worked up the narrow trail with the marshal, reaching the top and laying him down gently.

"The others couldn't help but hear that," Glencoe grunted. "Don't stop here. I don't think a man could go down there and come out alive with all of them waiting, Kennison, but if you do, we'll just forget that prison break. Damned technicality, anyway, seeing as it wasn't you who shot Marshal Peterson. You didn't have any business in that jail in the first place. Damned technicality. . . ."

Kennison took off Glencoe's faded bandanna and wadded it beneath the man's shirt, trying to staunch the flow of blood. Glencoe groaned, waved him away. Kennison's face was set and pale when he arose. For almost as long as he could remember now, he had closed himself off from feelings like this, forcing himself into a cold, deliberate, calculating mold because a man lived longer in his business if he didn't leave any room for emotion. But now it was like tearing a part out of him to leave Glencoe lying there, breathing so faintly, face so white.

He turned suddenly and moved down the other side of the escarpment, taking the right branch of the path where it forked at the boulder, because even fifteen years ago, when his half-brother had brought him up here and tried to force him in with the Bunch, that left fork of the trail had been dangerous.

They had heard the shots, all right. Kennison reached the timber when the sound of someone's running through the canoe birch came from ahead of him. He ducked to the right, going fast, bent over. He passed through the thick stand of gleaming white trunks and broke into the open and almost ran head-on into the Labarges.

"It's Kennison!" shouted Colonel Jack Labarge, and kept coming right on in a heavy-footed run, jerking his gun up.

"Saratoga! Over this way! It's Kennison!"

His six-shooter flamed before he finished shouting, and flamed again, and then Kennison's single, deliberate shot caught Colonel Jack and spun him around and dropped him on his face with a sodden sound.

Endee Labarge had been running behind his father. He tried to stop himself, stumbling sideways, both his fancy Colts hammering wildly. Kennison had marked Endee for that kind from the first and had seen men shoot that way too often before—emptying their guns as fast as they could squeeze the triggers, without waiting to get in range or taking aim. It was incredible how many times they could miss.

With the wild lead humming around him and clattering through the trees behind, Kennison stopped just in front of Colonel Jack's body. Endee was running sideways and backward now, still shooting, tripping on his high boots and throwing his Colts down wildly on each shot. But his eyes were on Kennison's unhurried thumb as it deliberately eared back the hammer on that blue Iver Johnson. A strange, twisted look crossed Endee's face. He triggered out a last desperate shot with his right-hand gun. Then he dropped it suddenly, and let go his other weapon, and raised both his hands in the air desperately.

"No, Kennison!" he screamed. "My God, no! I'm through. Don't shoot, Kennison."

Kennison stood there with his cocked gun held level. The abject fear in the man filled him with a momentary disgust. He moved across the glade toward Endee.

"The girl?" he asked.

"In the shack," babbled Endee. "Don't shoot. . . ."

It was a brutal thing to do, but for fifteen years Kennison had lived by expediency, and he couldn't take this man along with him, or leave him here. When he reached Endee, he caught one of his upraised arms suddenly, spinning the surprised man around. Endee hadn't yet made an outcry when Kennison's gun barrel struck him behind the head.

It was the clearing, then. Kennison realized he would be a fool to burst into the open. This would be playing into Saratoga's hands, giving him every advantage. The intelligent thing to do would have been to stay in the timber and draw Saratoga out, or wait for nightfall. But all Kennison could think of was the girl in the cabin. And somehow, his mind stopped, and he skirted around behind the cabin where there were no windows and burst from the trees in a hard, bent-forward run.

He got around in front of the cabin and ducked beneath the window on the right-hand side. He picked up a rock and flung it in through the open door. It bounced across the floor, and stopped. There was no other sound.

He took a breath and went in with a rush. The front room was empty.

He picked up one of the rickety chairs and slung it through the door into the second room and followed it running. He jerked right and left going in, finger taut and white on the trigger. Then he stumbled and stopped, and stood beside the girl who lay tied and gagged in a bunk. Maybe she was the only one in there.

It had been a long time since Kennison had made that kind of a mistake. It had been a long time since he had allowed his emotions to sweep all his careful deliberation from him. But he had thought only of getting to Viola, and he saw the error now, and he heard the small, scraping sound from the outside that might have been a man's boot heels on the doorjamb.

Yet, looking down at her as he whirled to the door, he realized he wouldn't do it any differently if he had another chance, or a thousand other chances. He didn't go clear into the front room. He stopped when he saw the tall, lean, gray-haired man silhouetted in the outer doorway. Saratoga must have thought the Labarges had stopped Kennison. He had put his gun away.

Kennison wasn't going to let him talk. He stiffened, and his pale face was suddenly wooden.

"Remember the girl," said Saratoga, and the voice was soft and lazy, and it stopped Kennison with his hand clawed down at his side. "That's right, Kenny. Viola's directly behind you in the bunk. She'd sure get one of my slugs if I shot you there. Why don't you move over to the side? That's right, Kenny. Sort of fitting we should meet this way finally, isn't it? Even up. No bottles to hit me with. That's right . . . move over to the side."

It put Kennison on the defensive, talking like that. It gave Saratoga the first bid, and the man with first bid always has the edge, and now Saratoga had the edge, and he was using it up to the hilt, building Kennison's tension to the breaking point with that soft talk, and Kennison wanted to scream: *Go ahead, damn you, go ahead!*

"I came back from New Orleans when Labarge let me know that Judge Barber was in line to be nabbed," said Saratoga. "I guess we all came back, didn't we? Sort of a gathering of the clans. . . ."

A hundred times before that lazy voice had covered Saratoga's move, and, although Kennison was waiting for it and knew it was coming, it startled him, and he was the slow man. His whole being seemed to explode in a blind, spasmodic reaction, and he didn't know anything between the time his hand dove for his gun and the first stunning pain of Saratoga's slug, slamming him back against the wall. He must have gotten his Iver Johnson free. It went off in his hand, pointing toward the roof.

All the sensation was gone from his legs. He didn't realize he was falling till he saw the floor rushing up to meet his face. In that last instant, he jerked his gun level again and caught Saratoga's silhouette over its rear sight. Their weapons hammered together. He heard Saratoga's slug eat into the wall behind him.

It was Glencoe who stumbled in over Saratoga's body some eternity later. Kennison jerked his hand feebly toward the rear room. The marshal had to go along the wall and hold himself up by the mud-chinked logs.

The girl appeared with him after a time. She turned pale when she saw Saratoga and Kennison lying there. Between them, Glencoe and the girl got Kennison into a chair.

Kennison didn't feel very much like telling the girl about her father now. That would come later, and he knew she would take it with the same courage that had sent her out every day to take care of the Barber spread in place of her father when he thought Kid Hodge was trying to kill her. She boiled some water in a kettle over the fireplace and washed both Kennison's and Glencoe's wounds.

"Saratoga told me who you were, Kid Hodge," she said.

He made a vague gesture with his hand. "Look. I didn't want to come back. I got over wanting any vengeance while I was in jail. After I broke out, I tried to stay away from here. But there was something pulling me back always . . . like a criminal has to return to the scene of his crime. It was sort of ironic that Glencoe should send for me to guard Judge Barber's daughter. Ironic or not, I couldn't stay away any longer. I didn't know it was the Jackson Hole Bunch after you. I thought that was all over. Even when I did come, I meant to leave as soon as the job was done. But now. . . ."

"There's plenty of fat cattle and high grass and deep water around here for a man who wants to stay," she said. "I wasn't really laughing at you for wanting a spread. I guess I was just trying to goad some feelings from you. It's what a man *should* want."

"I'd like to stay," Kennison said. "But there's something more than just the cattle and the land. . . ."

"If you mean what I think you mean," she said, suddenly very absorbed in the bandage she was tying on his shoulder, "you'll find that here, too, whenever you want it."

"I'm glad we all understand one another then," said Kennison.

The girl looked up at him, and they did.

THE LONE STAR CAMEL CORPS

Although this short novel appeared in Fiction House's *Frontier Stories* in the issue dated Summer, 1945, it was actually written six months before "The Hangman's *Segundo*," published that same quarter in *Action Stories*. Les Savage, Jr.'s title for this story was "Camels for Jeff Davis." Savage's agent sent it to Fiction House where editor Malcolm Reiss bought it on June 27, 1944. Savage was paid $305.00, or 2¢ a word for an estimated 15,250 words. In 1955 Savage asked Fiction House for an assignment back to him out of the composite copyright for the issue of *Frontier Stories* in which "The Lone Star Camel Corps" had appeared. His novel in manuscript, NORTH TO KANSAS, had been universally rejected by book publishers in 1954 and 1955 because it narrated how a white man falls in love with a black slave girl who, after having escaped from her Cherokee Indian master, is being returned for a ransom and how the two of them subsequently come to marry while living as fugitives among the pro-Union Cherokees who neither owned plantations nor practiced slavery. In his revised manuscript Savage abandoned the slave girl in the seventh chapter and rewrote and expanded "The Lone Star Camel Corps" to make a new conclusion to the story—one sufficiently acceptable to Pocket Books, which published this bowdlerized version as an original paperback under the title ONCE A FIGHTER in April, 1956. NORTH TO KANSAS, as Les Savage, Jr., originally imagined it, will be published as a

Five Star Western in March, 2002. What follows is the original text of "The Lone Star Camel Corps" as Savage wrote it, retaining for its first book publication the title given to it by *Frontier Stories*.

I

D*AVY CROCKETT*, thought Corporal Eddie Carnahan, *must be turning over in his grave today. Yes, if the hero of the Alamo could see what they were unloading on the shores of his beloved Texas this June day of 1857, he would surely be turning over in his grave. Camels, by James Bowie's blade!*

"Carnahan!" bellowed Sergeant Maxeter. "If you came along just to watch this circus, you'd better take those stripes off your sleeve right now. Lend a hand with this son of Satan, or I'll have you on every K.P. detail from here to Californy."

Eddie Carnahan moved across Indianola's cement docks, feeling the weary anger rise inside him again. The antipathy that had existed between him and the sergeant from the beginning was a natural one. The rivalry between the muleskinners and cavalry had always been as intense as that between the cavalry and the infantry, and ever since Corporal Carnahan's troop had arrived in old Camp Verde a month ago to join Sergeant Maxeter's 'skinners on this crazy detail, the trouble between the two outfits had grown. Now, with a hard, sweaty, back-breaking day of unloading these recalcitrant camels behind him, Carnahan wondered how much longer he could take Maxeter's bullying.

It had been Jefferson Davis's idea. If camels were so successful in the deserts of Africa and the Near East, he had argued, why not on the Great American Desert? And in 1853, as Secretary of War, Davis had secured an appropriation from Congress of thirty thousand dollars for the experiment and had commissioned Major Henry C. Wayne in conjunction with Lieutenant Porter, commanding the naval store ship, *Supply*, to sail to Cairo and the Near East in search of the first contingent of camels. And here they were. *And here I am*, thought Corporal Eddie Carnahan bitterly, *stuck with the zaniest detail the Army had ever had*.

His body had a lithe, whiplash look in its sweaty blue denims with the canary yellow strips of the cavalry down the seams of his trousers. The somber melancholy of Erin was in his dark eyes and the lean intensity of his aquiline face, but it was belied by the promise of a smile hovering at one corner of his broad, facile mouth. He came to a stop at the foot of the gangway, reaching up a sinewy, brown hand to catch the dirty hemp bridling the camel's twitching snout.

Sergeant Maxeter had moved in from the other side, a squat, thick-bellied, crop-haired Teuton with the rumpled collar of his dirty shirt unbuttoned around his thick, red neck, and his big Army Colt shoved around to the middle of his back where it wouldn't get in the way. As important a part of the experiment as the camels themselves were the native drivers brought along to teach the American troopers how to handle the beasts. Farrid Kerem was on the gangplank to one side of the animal, a hawk-nosed Syrian who spoke no English, the whites of his eyes gleaming fiercely from a dark face, a robe of red-and-white stripes flapping at his leather sandals. The camel was a fawn-colored, one-humped animal, and Carnahan tried to gentle it across the bottom of the gangplank onto the cement. But it set long legs and threw up its quivering snout, a terrifying grunt rumbling up from one of its four stomachs.

"These things ain't any different from mules, Carnahan," growled Sergeant Maxeter impatiently. He stepped up beside the corporal, reaching for the bridle and giving a vicious tug. "Move, you dirty-hocked, hump-backed, cross-eyed seventh cousin to a calico mule. I'll pull your drooling chin off."

Another of the natives stood at the thwarts of the *Supply*, a fat little Turk named Hassan who wore a red fez to signify his pilgrimage to Mecca, and he shouted at Maxeter: "*Effendi*, you can't treat that one so. She is a *hejin*, a Thoroughbred. She is Raf-alla."

"Raf-alla, your dirty ears," brayed Maxeter, and wrenched the prod pole from Farrid Kerem. "She's nothing but a jackass with a hump, and I'll treat her like any jackass. . . ."

Carnahan leaped aside from the swinging pole as Maxeter brought it around in a vicious arc. It made a sickening *thwack* on the camel's side. The beast screamed and reared up, jerking from side to side and smashing against the railing on the gangplank.

"*Effendi!*" yelled Farrid Kerem, grabbing at Maxeter. "*Anlayor mi-sin?* Raf-alla. . . ."

Maxeter swung the pole back, catching the Syrian across his stomach. "Out of my way, you African coyote. I've had enough of your Raf-alla!"

The robed Syrian fell back against the broken rail, barely catching himself from falling over into the water. Maxeter beat at the camel again, hanging onto her bridle with one hand as she screamed and tried to jerk away. Farrid Kerem jumped back to his feet, dark face twisted with pain and rage.

"*Yallah!*" he screamed, and Carnahan caught the flash of a curved blade from beneath his red-and-white robe. "*Inshallah!*"

Maxeter released the bridle and dropped his pole and whirled to grab for his Colt all in one movement. Released, the frenzied camel emitted a gurgling bellow and reared up into the air directly above the sergeant.

"Maxeter!" shouted Carnahan, and was already throwing himself at the non-com.

It was point-blank range, and Maxeter couldn't have missed, even with the camel coming down on him. Face stamped with a blind rage, he had his gun out and leveled at the charging Syrian, and the only thing that saved Farrid was Carnahan's body, smashing into Maxeter from the side. The gun exploded into the air, and the two non-coms crashed over against the weakened railing. They went through with a crackling pop of broken wood, and, behind them, the gangplank shuddered violently as the camel's forepaws thundered down where Sergeant Maxeter had stood a moment before.

Carnahan was conscious of Maxeter's heavy, fetid body against him, then the sudden shock of cold water. He fought away from the man's flailing legs and began to breaststroke to stop his downward plunge. His lungs were bursting by the time he had frog-kicked to the surface. A pair of troopers was already hauling Maxeter out from the wooden quay at the stern of the *Supply*. Carnahan swam to the quay and grasped his way up onto the platform.

There was something ludicrous about Maxeter, standing up there at the top of the steps leading from the quay, sputtering and gasping and shaking himself like a dog, the denims clinging soggily to his thick torso. One of the troopers holding the struggling, cursing Farrid Kerem couldn't help grinning. The men who had helped Maxeter out were turned partly away, shoulders trembling suspiciously. The natives lining the thwarts of the *Supply* were laughing openly.

"You did that deliberately, Carnahan," said Maxeter, and his guttural voice shook with rage. "You've been looking for a chance ever since you hit Camp Verde. You did it on purpose."

Carnahan pawed dripping hair from his eyes. "But the driver was right about those camels, Sergeant. You can't treat them like mules. You saw what that. . . ."

"Shut up!" bellowed Maxeter, thick torso lunging forward. "This is my outfit. I'll handle it like I please, mules, horses, or men. You think I'll let a dirty little boots-and-saddles corporal come in and tell me how to do it. You've been laying for me, Carnahan. You've been waiting for a chance like this."

Carnahan shook his head. "Sergeant, that camel. . . ."

Maxeter took a sudden step forward. "Shut up. . . ."

"Sergeant Maxeter!"

The cool, precise voice stopped the sergeant right there. He stood for a long instant with that hairy ham of a hand raised beside Carnahan's head. Then he let it down slowly, and turned toward the slim, blond lieutenant who stood farther down the quay near the line of unloaded camels. Although Lieutenant Travis was officially in command of

63

the combined outfits of 'skinners and cavalry, he was a cavalryman himself, having come down with the squadron of the 7th to which Carnahan was attached. He wasn't long out of West Point, Travis, and his sense of responsibility set heavily upon the carefully composed lines of his thin, aristocratic face with its proud, beaked nose and sensitive mouth.

"That would have been court-martial, wouldn't it, Sergeant?" he said thinly. "Striking the corporal?"

Maxeter swabbed at his dripping face with a dirty cuff. "He knocked me off that. . . ."

"I saw what happened," said Lieutenant Travis. "That camel was coming down right on top of you. If that corporal hadn't knocked you aside, you wouldn't be standing here now, wet *or* dry." He hitched at his cavalry saber self-consciously, biting his lips as if coming to a decision. Then he nodded curtly. "Go on with the unloading. I'll want to see both of you after retreat this evening."

Maxeter stood rigidly, watching the lieutenant as he walked up the gangplank and down the inside of the *Supply*'s thwart to the cabin amidships where Major Wayne was clearing the manifest. The water in the sergeant's shoes made a squelching sound as he turned back toward Carnahan. His fists were clenched and his little, blue eyes were narrowed to mere slits. He spoke through his teeth.

"All right, Corporal. You heard him. Get back to work." His voice lowered to a hoarse, trembling rasp. "And don't think I'm forgetting this. It's been coming ever since they assigned you dog-robbers to this detail back at Camp Verde. It's a long way between here and Californy, Carnahan, and I'll make you crawl every foot of the way. I'll keep you down on your hands and knees with your face in the droppings, and I'll break you at the end, if it's the last thing I do!"

II

WHEN he had founded the town as a port of entry for German immigrants in 1844, Prince Carl Zu Solms-Brannfals had named it Carlshafen, but it had been changed to Indianola, turning into the busiest port on this section of the Gulf Coast. Twilight softened the squalor of the waterfront streets overlooking the waters of Matagorda Bay. After the sweaty work of the day, the cool breeze springing up off the Gulf was a welcome relief to Corporal Eddie Carnahan, walking down the quay south of where the *Supply* was moored, still smarting under the school-book reprimand Lieutenant Travis had given him and Maxeter.

He pushed through the slatted doors of the Lavaca Saloon, thirsty for some decent beer after the two percent swill the sutler's store at Camp Verde had foisted on the troops while they were stationed there. Several blue-coated, enlisted men stood at the bar, and one hung on the tinny piano by the potted plants to the rear of the room. All of them were 'skinners from Maxeter's detail, and they glanced at Carnahan with a momentary, thinly veiled hostility, and turned away to ignore him pointedly. He bellied up to the bar and was blowing foam off his drink, when the two civilians moved in beside him.

"Well, Dempewolff," he said, and finished with the

foam. "You're a long way from home."

Carl Dempewolff was the Southwest agent for Harris Shippers, which had maintained headquarters at Fort Bowie in Arizona while Carnahan had been there. He was a heavy-set, little man with muttonchop whiskers growing smugly from a pompous set of red jowls, his bloodshot eyes pouched with rich living. He tucked a fat thumb into the string of gold nuggets forming the watch chain that crossed the bed-of-flowers waistcoat, and lifted a plump leg to put a patent leather boot on the tarnished rail.

"Business brings me south, Corporal. Join Pannah and me in a drink?"

Carnahan had never been able to decide whether Pannah Parker was Indian or Mexican, or both. He wore a fringed jacket made from the hide of a pinto pony.

Carnahan glanced at Maxeter's men again, and maybe they were why he shrugged and followed Dempewolff to one of the deal tables at the rear of the saloon. At the fat man's nod, the barkeep had gone through a door behind the bar, and now he came out, carrying a Pinch bottle grayed with dust.

"Well," said Dempewolff, puffing himself into a rickety, reed-bottomed chair. "Lot different from Fort Bowie, eh? You still studying for an appointment at the Academy?"

"I was going to Officers' School until this detail came up," said the corporal, and he couldn't help the faint disgust in his tone.

Dempewolff chuckled. "Sort of makes you mad, eh? I don't blame you, Carnahan. Rotten deal. Cuts a big chunk out of your time. But it's not as crazy as it looks, Corporal." He began pouring the drinks. "No, not as crazy as it looks.

66

Camels? Everybody's laughing at poor old Jeff Davis, aren't they? Yeah. Very funny. Except those on the inside. Freighters, for instance, like Harris. And me. Jefferson Davis isn't as crazy as he seems. A very smart man, in fact. A man to watch. He'll be more than Secretary of War one of these days, mark my words."

Carnahan twirled his glass, studying the rich liquor. "I don't know. From what I've seen, those camels are even harder to handle than mules."

"All depends on how you handle them," chuckled Dempewolff. "That's the case in anything. All depends on how you handle it. Me, I've always used my brains. Get enough native drivers over here with those camels and you'd have the start of dangerous competition for the shippers working the desert routes now. Oh, don't laugh, Carnahan. That's where people make their mistake. Look. A Syrian camel can carry five hundred pounds some thirty-five miles in a twelve-hour day. Four Syrian camels equal the two thousand pound payload you can haul in a Conestoga. How does that compare with your wagon, drawn by mules or oxen? The best 'whacker east of the Missouri can't push a mule team over twenty miles in that length of that time, closer to fifteen on an average. That leaves your camel traveling twice as fast. And all you've got is four animals to a payload, where with your wagon rig you've got a Conestoga and maybe seven, eight spans of mules. Facts, Carnahan, figures. And what they add up to isn't a very pleasant outlook for the shippers, if this camel experiment is handled right."

Carnahan tossed off his drink, squinted his eyes, and tried to enjoy the smooth, oily fire coursing down his throat. But somehow he couldn't, and, when he opened his eyes again, they had taken on a dark intensity, because he was beginning to sense something behind Dempewolff's bland chuckle.

"Sort of hard," said Pannah Parker, spreading his fingers on the table, "sort of hard for an enlisted man to get an appointment to West Point."

"We were talking," said Carnahan, "about camels." His glass made an irritated clink when he set it down.

"Almost impossible," smiled Dempewolff, "almost impossible for an enlisted man."

"I think that depends on the man's ability," said Carnahan, almost angrily. "My C.O. thinks enough of my ability to give me a recommendation as soon as I finish Officer's School at Bowie."

"It would be much more effective to have your senator recommend you, wouldn't it?" said Dempewolff. "That's the usual procedure, isn't it? It takes pull to get that kind of recommendation, of course. It takes pull to get in the Academy any way you try it. Pull and influence. A lot of it."

"I don't think so," said Carnahan. "I think a man's ability. . . ."

"You aren't that naïve, Corporal," said Dempewolff. "You know about how much chance you stand of getting a commission the way you're trying to do it. One in a thousand? On the other side, however, there are certain interested parties who might get in touch with your senator . . . say, parties who have the necessary influence. They'd put so much grease on your track to a commission you wouldn't even feel the slide in."

"Interested parties?" said Carnahan.

"You're a smart boy," said Pannah Parker.

"As I said," nodded Dempewolff, "Jackson Harris is a foresighted man. He sees the detrimental effects an influx of these camels would have on our shipping business. This first trip you're taking to California is the experiment that will make or break Jefferson Davis's little plan. Public opinion is already so much against him that he'll never be able to get another appropriation through for more of his Arabian pets, if the camels show up unfavorably on this trek."

Carnahan almost knocked over his chair as he kicked it back and stood up. "Why come to me? Why not go straight to Lieutenant Travis? He's in command."

"Take it easy, boy," said Dempewolff, looking around. "Take it easy. Sit down. We decided the lieutenant was incorruptible. He already has a commission, and I'm afraid a man with four years of the Academy so recently behind him is filled with those stupid ideals they grope around in up there. You know. Besides, he's not experienced with the country you're taking those camels through. You are, Carnahan. I understand you come from this part of Texas. Anything that befell those camels under your ministrations would look very natural. They just didn't work out, see. Maybe the Great American Desert was too rocky for their feet and cut them all up. Or maybe the graze made them sick. I wouldn't know. You would. You'd know. And when it's all over, the public have had their last little laugh, and Jefferson Davis's idea didn't work out, and Harris Shippers continues to operate its business as before, and one Corporal Eddie Carnahan becomes Lieutenant Carnahan, and all his friends call him Mister."

Carnahan's face darkened. He started to say something,

then he shoved his chair on back and turned toward the door with a jerk. He had taken one step when Pannah Parker was there, somehow, rising and slithering into his way with a swift, snake-like movement.

"Going, Corporal?" asked Parker.

Carnahan stiffened with the feel of Dempewolff's hand on his arm and the smooth, unctuous sound of the man's voice in his ear. "You don't want to be hasty, Carnahan. There could be more than just a commission in it for you. An officer's pay isn't too large, any way you look at it. As Harris's agent there at Bowie, I could supplement it from time to time when you came back there with the bars on your shoulders."

Carnahan could feel the hot flush in his taut, intense face, and his voice trembled slightly with his restraint. "What do you think I am, Dempewolff, another Benedict Arnold? I don't want any of your rotten money. Take your hands off me!"

The piano had stopped, and the troopers at the bar had turned to look. Under any other circumstances, Dempewolff would have been surrounded by bluecoats, already coming to Carnahan's aid. But these were Maxeter's men, and they watched almost eagerly, and Pannah Parker smiled faintly, putting a slick-tipped finger up to stroke the collar of Carnahan's coat.

"Like Carl says, don't be too hasty. There's another side of the picture."

"I'm not going to ask you again," said Carnahan, and his voice held the same ferine intensity as his lean face now. "Take your hands off and let me by."

"Yes," said Dempewolff. "Another side to the picture. We

have the influence to make things very nice for you, if you take our offer the right way. We also have the influence to make things rather nasty. Remember Sergeant Field? Must be two years since he blew his brains out up there at Apache. I often wonder if he didn't muff a chance somewhere along the line, or cross somebody he shouldn't have crossed. . . ."

"Damn you!"

Almost screaming it, Carnahan whirled, tearing Dempewolff's hand off his arm. He hooked a sinewy fist into the man's pudgy belly, saw Dempewolff crash backward into the table, upsetting it. Carnahan whirled back and leaped at Pannah Parker. The man had taken a step back to draw, and his gun was already out when Carnahan hit him. The Blunt and Symms exploded into the air, hot lead whipping past Carnahan's ear as his forearm knocked the gun barrel on up. Then he was straddled on Pannah Parker, letting all the pent-up anger of the day explode in the fist he smashed against the man's thin face.

Parker's head snapped back beneath the blow and hit the splintery floor with a sharp, hollow sound. Then there was a hoarse shout, and the scuffle of boots behind Carnahan. He was half risen when the first blow struck the back of his neck.

His body flinched to a foot, smashing against his ribs, and sick pain blinded him. The rifle butt struck his head while he was rolling over feebly, and the foot caught him in the ribs again, rolling him back. He heard his own agonized gasp.

"All right, all right," said a voice he knew well enough. "That'll do. We don't want him to die before we reach Californy, do we?"

Through the haze of agony, Carnahan opened his eyes. Sergeant Maxeter stood above him, with two armed guards. In that moment Carnahan wondered if the sergeant hadn't been following him, waiting for the first break like this.

"Assault?" said Maxeter, looking down at Carnahan. "Civilian, too. This'll go bad for you, Corporal. Might even lose your stripes. A couple of weeks' fatigue duty either way"—his grin was suddenly very ugly—"and this is only the beginning, Carnahan, believe me, only the beginning."

III

CORPORAL CARNAHAN eased himself around in his hard McClellan saddle and looked back at the line of camels strung out behind him, disappearing into the haze that had swept in off the Gulf during the afternoon. They were making evening camp outside San Antonio, while Lieutenant Travis made his report to General Baylor commanding the Department of Texas, prior to striking out on the first real leg of the trail to Fort Tejon, California.

The caravan had a dual purpose, the primary one being to test the camels on a protracted march, the other to survey a military road from Zuñi to the Colorado River. Although the troop of cavalry to which Carnahan was attached had been detailed to break in some of the camels for riding, Lieutenant Travis seemed hesitant about mounting them. Watching the lumbering beasts plod past him now, Carnahan didn't blame the lieutenant much; he wasn't too eager to climb aboard these strange ships of the desert himself.

Travis let his long-legged gray drop back from the head of the line. "Don't forget you're on fatigue tonight, Corporal. After the camels it's K.P. till seven. Horse lines till twelve. No more trouble, Carnahan?"

Carnahan turned toward him. "Lieutenant, I tried to tell you last night. . . ."

"I'd rather not hear," said Travis stiffly. "You were a little incoherent last night. The only thing that saved you from losing your stripes was your previous record. Now, Carnahan, you'll serve out your penalty, and we'll forget the matter."

"But I've got to tell you what Dempewolff. . . ."

"I told you to forget it," said Travis hotly. "Don't make things worse for yourself. You know Texas better than all the rest of us put together, and I need you and I've tried to be lenient with you on that account. Now let's oblique the line."

He spurred his gray ahead, and Carnahan sat looking after him for a moment, lean body rigid as a Sharps ramrod. Then he gigged his roach-maned cavalry mount in close to the line of camels. The native driver nearest him was Lidea Kerem, a Syrian youth who was the brother of Farrid Kerem, and who wore a long, richly embroidered gown of white cotton and a coat of dark, red stripes over that. On his head was a cap of black velvet, bound around and around with silver coils, and upon that was draped a burnoose of yellow silk that half hid his dark face. Carnahan had learned that Lidea spoke English better than the others, and he leaned from the saddle, waving a chevroned arm toward the dark blot of Mission San Juan Capistrano, eastward from the Espada Road.

"We're making camp down by the river tonight. Start turning your camels on past that mission."

Lidea Kerem's eyes flashed darkly from beneath the

burnoose, and the size of them was startling. *"Ai, effendi."*

Forty-one camels out beyond the Sibley tents. Forty-one grumbling, groaning, spitting, shaggy, intractable beasts to unload of their burdens. Forty-one obstinate, perverse devils to haul and yank and pull down to the San Antonio River and water and haul and yank and pull back to the bed ground. Helping Carnahan was the Turk named Hassan, a jolly, little man in a red fez and baggy, blue pants belted around his extensive circumference with a tasseled, velvet rope. Carnahan had caught the hemp bridle of a double-humped Bactrian camel and was pulling it into line. He grimaced suddenly, almost gagging, turning his face away sharply. Hassan chuckled.

"Ai, effendi, you came in from the wrong side that time. Always stay to the windward of these *oonta*. Their essence is hardly *eau de cologne*, eh? With all their faults, however, one can learn to love them like a woman. They are really remarkable beasts. Did you ever see another animal, for instance, that can boast four stomachs? Or such a long neck? And in battle, by the beard of Allah, you should see them in battle! Bullets seem to have no effect on them, *effendi*. I saw my father bring in a gray *hejin* once, after a raid on the Arabs, and we counted forty-four bullet holes in the beast."

"That's hard to believe," said Carnahan.

"I suppose so," said Hassan. "But it is true. Forty-four bullets, and the *hejin* didn't seem bothered at all. It is very accountable, of course. The camel's hump is all gristle and fat. You could shoot him there all day and he would hardly feel it. And with four stomachs, you can fill three of them

74

with lead and still leave him enough digestive apparatus to live quite comfortably, eh?" He slapped his fat thigh, laughing. "Just because he has such a singular capacity for lead, though, doesn't mean he is so tough otherwise. You have to treat him gently, *effendi. Ai.* Don't start loading him while he's standing. Tell him to *barrak.*"

Carnahan grinned. *"Barrak?"*

The camel curled its hair lip and stayed on its long legs, and Hassan chortled. "Louder, *effendi*, more authority. *Barrak*, you son-of-a-dog, *barrak!"*

Carnahan jumped away, as the camel emitted a rumbling belch, spattering him with its foul, green cud. But the animal began lowering itself to knobby fore knees. That was as far as it had gotten when Carnahan heard Sergeant Maxeter down the line. The sergeant was leading a string of mules, singing the only song he knew in his guttural, toneless, off-key monotone.

> Oh, I'd like to be a packer, and pack with
> George F. Crook,
> And dressed up in my canvas suit, I'd be
> for him mistook. . . .

The first lop-eared mule had lifted twitching nostrils, and Hassan shouted at Maxeter. "Take your mules to the windward, *effendi*. They go crazy when they smell the camels."

But Maxeter either didn't hear him, or ignored him.

The mule suddenly got the full effect of the camel's singularly foul odor and began to lunge on the lead line, kicking and braying. They dated the strange appearance of so many deaf jackasses in Arizona from the time Sergeant

Maxeter came to Fort Bowie, and he did justice to his reputation now, letting out a string of expletives that raised the camel's head with a sharp jerk. But the mules were in a frenzy. One of them smashed into his mate, ripping loose both their *aparejos* and spilling collapsed Sibley tents from the packsaddles. Hoofs shredding the canvas, one of the maddened mules charged the camel. The Bactrian lurched clumsily off his fore knees and turned to bite the mule with a savage scream.

"Beard of the Prophet," shouted Hassan. "*Hyah*, you son-of-a-*djinn. Hyah, hoosh. Hoosh!*"

"Carnahan, help me with these pack asses! Leave that camel be," brayed Maxeter. "Whoa, you lop-eared cousin to an inbred polecat. Gee! Haw! Carnahan . . . !"

Knocked aside by the plunging camel, Carnahan ran head-on into one of the mules. Reeling back, he grabbed wildly at the lead rope, hauling the frenzied beast down. Troopers were running in from the horse lines. A camel had broken loose farther on down, and it charged through the mêlée, long neck snaking from one side to the other as it took a vicious nip at everything it passed.

"*Hyah. Hoosh. Hoosh!*"

It took them an hour to restore order. Travis finally issued four-hour passes to the muleskinners, and they left for San Antone. The lieutenant left shortly afterward to report to the department commander in town, several miles up the river. Carnahan was making his rounds at the south end of the horse lines when the shadowy figure materialized from behind a sleepy gray.

"Halt . . . !"

"It's Lidea Kerem," said the youth, and Carnahan recognized Farrid's brother. The boy came closer, a suppressed excitement in his voice. "*Effendi*, that Sergeant Maxeter has taken most of the native drivers into the city."

"Maxeter?" said Carnahan. "I thought he didn't like you?"

"He hates us," said Lidea Kerem. "That's just it. I'm afraid, *effendi*. That sergeant has the Evil Eye. He's up to no good. If you'll only come with me and bring them back. I can't do anything alone. They wanted to see San Antone. The lieutenant is gone. You are the only one left with authority."

"But I'm confined to camp," said Carnahan. "I'd lose my stripes if they caught me outside. What about Corporal O'Malley?"

"Maxeter's man," spat the Syrian youth. "Why even ask him?"

O'Malley was at one of the campfires near the end of the line of Sibleys, a tall, red-haired non-com with freckled, bony hands and a raucous voice that came to a man who spent his life shouting at mules. As Carnahan approached, O'Malley stood up, something stiff and hostile about his awkward movements, and the talk around the fire ceased.

"I'd like to speak with you, O'Malley."

"Whatever you have to say can be said here," said the 'skinner.

Carnahan shook his head angrily. "All right, then. Your sergeant has taken the native drivers into town, and he's up to no good. You know how he hates them. If he gets them drunk, there's no telling what'll happen. You've got to go and bring them back."

"Got to?" O'Malley sneered it.

"Yes," said Carnahan tensely. "Forget our personal differences for now. If anything happens to those drivers, this experiment might as well be stuffed in your blanket roll. We can't handle the camels without those natives. Quit thinking of yourself, O'Malley. Maybe you 'skinners don't like the camels. Well, neither do I. But its a job we're given to do. You've done other jobs, tougher ones. If you were ordered to charge a tribe of Blackfeet with an empty breechloader, you'd do it. I know."

O'Malley deliberately squatted down again. "Go feed that hay to the horses."

"No," said Carnahan. "If you let this detail down, you're letting the Army down. It's our job. Maxeter's up to something, and you've got to stop him. I'll take over here while you go into town."

"You'll take over!" O'Malley laughed, and the other 'skinners joined in. "You'll take over in the guardhouse if you don't get back to your post. I'm in command here, Carnahan. You're on fatigue, and I'm in command, and I'm ordering you to shut your knapsack and get back to the horse lines. On the double!"

Carnahan stood there for a moment with his hands opening and closing. Then he turned and walked away from the Sibleys.

"I have mounts, *effendi*, outside camp. . . ."

Carnahan became aware that the Syrian boy had been with him all this time. He stopped there in the darkness. Maxeter. The name goaded him. He turned to Lidea Kerem with a sharp, decisive movement, and the youth's smile gleamed faintly in the darkness.

"There are still several of the older drivers left here in

camp. They will divert your sentries while we slip through."

The shifting movement in the *álamos* by the river was the first sign Carnahan had. The three camels threw their shadows, long and sombrous, over the moonlit water.

"You said mounts . . . ?"

"These are mounts," said Lidea. "We would have been stopped trying to get horses out of camp. Hassan told the sentries he was watering these camels. Are you afraid, *effendi* . . . ?"

"No, but camels. . . ."

The Turk named Hassan was holding the animals. "You have seen only the *djemel-mais, effendi*, the double-humped Bactrians from Persia, which are used as pack animals. These are *hejins*. Dromedaries."

Carnahan had begun to notice that they were smaller than the animals he had worked with this afternoon, and that they only had one hump. The fawn-colored hair was short and fine, and Carnahan moved closer, sniffing.

The Turk chuckled. "*Ai*, these do not smell like our old *djemel-mais*, eh? There are as many breeds of camel as there are of horses, and these Arabians are the finest Thoroughbreds in the world."

"*Hejin*, you said?" muttered Carnahan. "That's what Farrid was shouting about when we had trouble on the gangway in Indianola."

Lidea Kerem laid a caressing hand on the finely arched neck of the nigh animal. "Of course. This is Raf-alla, the one Sergeant Maxeter was beating at Indianola. She is Farrid's own racing dromedary. Do you wonder he attacked the sergeant when Maxeter did that to Raf-alla?

Maybe you kick a mule, *effendi*, but would you kick your favorite horse? Would you let anyone else kick him? Now, we must hurry. *Barrak*, Raf-alla, *barrak*."

The *hejin* knelt, and, somewhat hesitantly Carnahan climbed on. The saddle wasn't unlike his McClellan, except there were no stirrups and the pommel and cantle were much higher. He leaned forward for the reins, and Hassan and Lidea Kerem mounted.

"*Goom*," Lidea called. "Raf-alla, *goom*."

Carnahan was jerked violently backward as the *hejin* rose with a lurch to its fore knees, then he was thrown forward, clutching wildly at the animal's neck as the rump heaved up. With back legs straightened fully, the beast rose from its fore knees, and Carnahan was thrown backwards again. Then the camel was erect, and Carnahan pulled in tightly on the reins without thinking. The dromedary shied and reared, and Carnahan slackened up, calling himself an ass.

At first, sitting so high filled him with a strange dizziness, and he had to hang onto the hand-tooled leather of the pommel to keep from falling. But when he got used to that, he was surprised at the easy, flowing gait the beast had slipped into, similar to that of a Kennedy Walker, only much smoother.

"Grip with your knees," said Hassan. "You are a horseman. It is not much different. Those *djemel-mais* are a terror to ride, but a racing dromedary is like floating, eh?"

"It is," said Carnahan.

ONE of the oldest cities in Texas, San Antonio was spread out on both banks of the river, a sprawling cluster of adobe houses lining narrow streets that radiated from the Álamo

Plaza in the center of town. They left the animals with the fat little Turk in the river bottoms south of the main part of town, well screened by a motte of shadowy cottonwoods. Carnahan led up Álamo Street, the crowds growing larger as he neared the plaza. There were many troopers, because the Department Headquarters was stationed here, but none from the corporal's 7th. In the flapping robes, Lidea Kerem passed for one of the countless blanketed Indians.

Shadowy figures filled the night cloaking the Álamo Plaza, passing back and forth in front of the crumbling, ivy-covered walls of the chapel where Davy Crockett and Colonel Bowie and so many others had fought to the last for Texas. Carnahan moved down Houston Street, more running than walking. The Buckhorn had been another of Maxeter's haunts, standing on the southwest corner of Houston and Flores. Carnahan was passing beneath the pin oak overhang of a dry goods store along Flores opposite from the saloon when the sound of his boots suddenly turned to a sharp scuffle, and he caught Lidea Kerem. He dragged the youth into the deeper shadows.

"May the hand of Fatima guard you," muttered Lidea.

Carnahan was staring intently across the intersection of Flores and Houston. "What?"

"The hand of Fatima," said the Syrian youth. "She was Mohammed's daughter. She guards the faithful from harm. That Sergeant Maxeter has the Evil Eye."

Maxeter stood on the opposite corner of the crossing, with two other men. One had pompous, red jowls sporting smug, muttonchop whiskers. Carl Dempewolff. Beside him stood the inevitable Pannah Parker, the peculiar slouch of his lean figure emanating a nervous viciousness.

"I thought there was something wrong about Maxeter's taking your men into town," said Carnahan, "but this is one I never figured on."

Maxeter said something in a thick, angry voice to Dempewolff and turned away to walk north on Flores, the plank walk shuddering beneath his quick, angry steps. Dempewolff watched him go a minute, then he turned to Pannah Parker with a chuckle, and the two of them crossed Houston toward the Buckhorn, disappearing through slatted doors into the saloon. Carnahan had started toward the Buckhorn, because he sensed what was coming. But before he was across Flores, there was a loud gunshot from inside the saloon, and the crash of broken glass, and the yellow square of a back window suddenly became a dark blot. Then a yell rose into the night, a strange, feral, wailing yell that sent a chill through Carnahan.

"Farrid," gasped Lidea Kerem, and began running ahead of the corporal, robes flapping.

Carnahan caught up with the Syrian boy as a man burst out through the batwing doors, face white. He careened into Carnahan and stumbled on out into the street. Then the corporal was inside, charging against a press of struggling, shouting, howling, shooting men.

That strange yell shook the rafters again. Carnahan saw it was the huge Syrian, Farrid Kerem, backed up against the bar and struggling like a trapped panther with half a dozen Mexicans and white men. The other tribesmen were answering the war cry, fighting their way from the rear part of the big room, where it had been thrown into darkness when the light was shot out.

Carnahan caught a greasy *peon* by the scruff of his neck

and levered him aside, elbowing on in toward the Syrian. With a prodigious effort, Farrid Kerem threw his attackers off momentarily and, placing his hands on the bar, vaulted to its top. Standing there with his legs spread, he swept the gleaming scimitar from beneath his red-and-white striped robes.

"Infidels!" he screamed, hacking at the men surging at him. "*Domuz!*"

A thrown bottle struck his head. He staggered, caught himself, thrusting with his sword at the man who tried to jump onto the bar. The man screamed and fell back, clutching at his shoulder as the blade slipped back out.

"Farrid!" yelled Lidea Kerem, fighting a way through the crowd in front of Carnahan, and Carnahan thought the boy's voice unusually shrill. "Farrid, stop it. Stop . . . !"

"Infidels, *fellahs* . . . !"

The other native drivers had fought their way toward the front, and an Arab was trying to get onto the bar farther down, kicking free of the Mexicans who caught at him. The barkeep tried to pop up from beneath his sill and pull Farrid off. The fierce Syrian whirled and put a sandal in his face, and whirled back to swing his deadly scimitar as the barkeep staggered back against his shelves, knocking down a row of bottles.

Carnahan butted his way through the crowd, catching a six-foot cowpuncher around his rawhide waist and heaving him aside, smashing a fist into the mustaches of a big Mexican muleteer. He almost fell beneath the man who reeled back from the bar, blood from Farrid's deadly blade spurting out of a gaping wound. Then Carnahan went head first to the bar beside Lidea Kerem and caught at Farrid, trying to pull him off.

"Are you crazy? We've got to get out of here. They'll kill you!"

Farrid kicked him in the face. Spitting blood, Carnahan bellied over the bar and rose to his hands and knees on the mahogany beside Farrid. The robed Syrian whirled toward him, sword whipping up. Farrid's dark face was twisted with rage, and his eyes were glazed with battle lust, and the blade hung in mid-air above his head for that instant, and Carnahan couldn't tell whether he would strike or not.

A flurry of shots broke out, and the mirror splintered into a thousand tinkling shards. Then the Arab driver who had climbed onto the bar came running down toward Farrid. There was another shot.

"Farrid," gasped the Arab, and staggered forward and fell against the Syrian, clutching at his robes and sliding down his body till he lay huddled across the bar.

With his sword still up in the air, Farrid turned back the other way. Still on his hands and knees across the bar, Carnahan could see it, too. At the other end of the scarred mahogany strip stood Pannah Parker. His Blunt and Symms was smoking, and he had it up by his ear to throw down on the next shot, and that would be Farrid's.

Carnahan's left hip was toward that end of the bar, and the Army packed its iron on that side. Knowing a draw would be too late, the corporal jammed his right hand across his belly and clawed the flap off his holster. He saw Pannah Parker's gun flashing down. Then his fingers were jammed into the holster, and he twisted his hand so far he thought he had broken the wrist, and the holster flopped outward.

The bellow of their guns sounded simultaneously to Carnahan. But Parker's shot must have been an instant later than the corporal's, and Carnahan's bullet must have struck Parker's gun as he fired, because Parker's slug crashed into the broken mirror above and behind Farrid, and Parker fell forward onto the bar, then slid off, and disappeared from Carnahan's view.

Farrid turned down to where Carnahan still crouched, supported by his left hand, his right arm held across his belly with his hand jammed into his holster and his fingers gripping the Colt inside, and the faint shred of gray powder smoke curling from the burned hole at the bottom of the holster. A surprised look crossed the rage in Farrid's face, and then he grinned.

"*Dostoum*," he said, and then what was probably the only English word he knew. "Friend."

But the crowd had surged up toward them in that instant, and men were swarming up to the bar and pulling at Farrid again, and their weight against Carnahan's legs almost forced him off. The corporal jerked his gun out and kicked free of the clawing hands, whirling to club at the black head of a Mexican who was on the bar. Farrid screamed wildly again, and his sword swung in that lethal arc, and the crowd fell back in front of him. Lidea Kerem was climbing onto the bar now, pulling at his brother. Carnahan caught the giant Syrian by his robes, trying to yank him away, but Farrid was swept with that blind lust for battle again.

"Stop it, you fool!" shouted Carnahan. "We've got to get out."

Then he saw the first M.P. burst into the room through the slatted doors. Farrid fought Carnahan off, a backward swipe of his blade ripping the corporal's sleeve from wrist to elbow. In desperation, Carnahan caught the man's burnoose with one hand and struck hard with his clubbed gun. Farrid stiffened, and slumped forward.

"*Effendi*," gasped the Arab that Pannah Parker had shot. He pawed weakly at Carnahan, trying to rise. "*Effendi. . . .*"

"I'll take care of Jemel," shouted Lidea Kerem. "You get my brother off there."

Kicking at the clawing hands, Carnahan heaved Farrid's bulk onto his shoulders in a fireman's carry.

The rear door gave onto a back room. Carnahan stumbled through the darkened place, tripping over the upset table and smashed oil lamp. Behind him, the saloon rocked to the din, and another flurry of shots followed him out the back portal into an alley.

Farrid was coming to, and Carnahan set him on his feet, driving him from the alley out toward Flores Street. Lidea Kerem and another tribesman were supporting the wounded man between them, and two other drivers followed, robes ripped, faces bloody.

The riot had drawn the crowds around to the front of the Buckhorn, and Flores was empty as far south as the Military Plaza. The seven turned west on Dolorosa and then north on Soledad to the alley that formed an easement to the San Antonio River. Farrid struggled feebly as Carnahan shoved him into the narrow way. Then the corporal turned to help them with the wounded man. He stopped with his hands outstretched, and in the darkness his face was a pale blot of surprise.

The silken burnoose and velvet cap had been torn from Lidea Kerem's head, and the lustrous hair that was released fell softly about the shoulders of the rich coat, and way down beneath his stunned surprise Carnahan suddenly realized that he had never seen such a beautiful girl in all his life.

IV

ORPORAL EDDIE CARNAHAN stood at rigid attention in Lieutenant Travis's wall tent, thumbs stiffly against the yellow stripes down the seams of his trousers. Maxeter was there, the flickering candle casting its yellow glow over his sullen, unshaven face. The lieutenant sat at his portable table, and the only sound for a long time had been the monotonous tap of his pencil against the table top.

It was the evening after the trouble at the Buckhorn. Carnahan had gotten the natives back into camp by the San Antonio River without being caught by the sentries and had been in his Sibley when Lieutenant Travis returned from San Antonio. The girl had pleaded with Carnahan not to reveal her secret, but he knew it was his duty and the next morning had approached Travis. The lieutenant had seemed in a great hurry to break camp and told Carnahan whatever he had to say could wait till later.

The lieutenant's pencil stopped its soft monotony, suddenly, and Travis looked up at Carnahan. His voice was carefully impersonal. "I'm disappointed in you, Corporal. When I asked for you back at Bowie, it wasn't only because you were familiar with this country, but because I thought you were one of the best non-coms the post had to offer on a detail of this nature. Being one of my men, I suppose I let myself be prejudiced in your favor when you had that trouble with Sergeant Maxeter while we were unloading the camels. I attributed the blame more to him than you. I'm beginning to think I was mistaken. You didn't help matters any by your conflict in the Lavaca Saloon. Drunken. Disorderly. Assault. What's gotten into you, Carnahan?"

"I wasn't drunk at the Lavaca," said Carnahan. "Every time I've tried to tell you what happened there, you wouldn't listen. And this morning, I tried to tell you about. . . ."

"About the girl?" asked Travis coldly.

Carnahan felt the surprise widen his dark eyes. "You know?"

Travis nodded. "I know about the girl. And I know about Dempewolff and Pannah Parker. Apparently the Harris Shippers are interested in seeing that this camel experiment is a failure. Is that connected with the trouble at the Buck-horn last night?" He waved his slim hand. "Oh, don't bother to protest. We haven't any proof that you were there, but we're not stupid, Carnahan."

"One of the M.P.s swears he saw Pannah Parker in the Buckhorn," said Maxeter. "Dead."

"Yes," said Travis, watching Carnahan narrowly. "A lot of the rioters were hacked up, and what few were arrested told garbled stories that weren't worth a dog robber's buttons. Nothing has been proved yet. This M.P. was chasing a bunch of rioters out the back of the saloon when he stumbled across the body at the end of the bar. Dempewolff and Parker had been dickering for a shipping contract from the Department of Texas and were known to the military in San Antonio, and the M.P. swears the dead man was Pannah

Parker. The M.P. chased the rioters out back, lost them on Flores Street. When he came back, Pannah Parker's body was gone. That was the only thing that saved us. I don't know who disposed of it. Dempewolff, maybe, or the barkeep. Whoever it was doesn't matter. With a murder on their hands, the department would have held our column there for the inquest. Weeks. Maybe months. We were just lucky. But if Parker was there, too, Carnahan . . . why?"

"If the drivers hadn't escaped," said Maxeter, "they would have been killed by that mob."

"Which would have finished the camel experiment at its beginning," said Travis. "I have an idea that whoever took the drivers into town did it with that very purpose in mind. Those natives didn't go of their own accord. Who took them, Carnahan? Why was Dempewolff at the Buckhorn?"

"I tried to tell you that Dempewolff approached me at the Lavaca, but you wouldn't listen," said Carnahan. "Dempewolff offered me help getting a commission if I'd cut the hobbles on this experiment. I refused."

"Did you?" said Travis insidiously. "Did you, Carnahan? Then who took the drifters into town?"

Carnahan looked at Maxeter and realized that if it came to his word against the sergeant's, Travis would be prejudiced the other way now. "Why don't you ask the natives?" he said stiffly.

"I wouldn't believe one of those drivers any more than I'd believe a dirty Indian," said Travis, tapping his pencil against the table. "They all swear they weren't in San Antonio last night. The wounded Arab named Jemel says he got the hole through his ribs cleaning a gun. They aren't supposed to have arms in the first place, and I couldn't find any gun in his. . . ." He threw the pencil down suddenly, moving his head from side to side impatiently. "Oh, why even discuss it? Nothing can be proved. I hate to think you'd be in with Dempewolff. I'd even be willing to take your word for it if it wasn't for this last bit of business. Why didn't you report the girl when you first discovered her in Indianola?"

"I didn't know about her till last night," said Carnahan.

"Didn't you?" said Travis, and his voice held soft disbelief.

Carnahan looked at Maxeter. "What's he been telling you?"

Travis stiffened. "The sergeant has done nothing but his duty. He reported the girl to me this evening. You should have come to me the instant you found out."

"I tried to tell you," said Carnahan desperately.

"I'm not talking about this morning," said Travis, and he shoved his chair back, standing up. "I should have done this after the Lavaca, I suppose. Now I'm not even going through the formality of a summary. This has been your court-martial. If I could prove you were connected with Dempewolff, I'd put you in irons. As it stands, you have been charged with, and found guilty of, striking your superior on the gangway at Indianola, drunken and disorderly at the Lavaca Saloon, assault, breaking confinement last night to engage in a riot in San Antone, concealing the identity of a person who doesn't officially belong to the caravan. Give me your stripes, Corporal Carnahan."

For a moment, Carnahan didn't move, and his face went white, and his mind was blank from the shock of it. Then, unaccountably, it wasn't anger that first seeped back, but memories. Vague, confused, poignant memories of all the sweat and pain and labor and battle that had gone into those stripes, the years of N.C.O. School at Fort Bowie, the stink of stables and fetid heat of barracks and freezing chill of winter marches. All wiped away in an instant by this slim, supercilious jackass from the Academy, saying: "Give me your stripes, Carnahan."

With a small, strangled sound, Carnahan reached up and ripped the chevrons from his blue sleeve. He wasn't looking at Travis when he handed them over. Travis spoke stiffly. "All right, Private Carnahan. You'll still serve out your former penalty. We aren't striking any military posts between here and Santa Fé, and your fatigue will last till then."

Carnahan hardly recognized his own voice. "Santa Fé? What about Fort Concho, and Apache?"

Travis dropped the torn chevrons onto the table, speaking impatiently. "I've changed the route. We were taking the shorter march past Concho and Apache because you knew the country. I was depending on your guidance across the badlands between the headwaters of the Nueces and Fort Concho. But now . . ."—he shrugged—"how can I depend on you for anything?"

"But it's the only logical route," said Carnahan, forgetting his stripes in that moment. "Up the Nueces and across the stretch between that and Fort Concho is almost a straight line."

"And almost all badlands, as bad as, if not worse, than the Devil's River route," said Travis, "so Maxeter tells me."

"Oh," said Carnahan. "So Maxeter tells you."

"In view of what's happened," said Travis, "I'm afraid

we'll have to strike west to Devil's River. From all reports, it runs some sixty miles or so farther north than the Nueces, and that would leave the stretch between its headwaters and New Mexico much shorter than the march between the head of the Nueces and Fort Concho."

"From whose reports?" said Carnahan bitterly. "Maxeter's? Sure, Devil's River runs farther north than the Nueces. But those sixty miles at its end are all dry bed. The sinkhole the Comanches call Beaver Lake is the last permanent water south of the Concho River. You'll have eighty, ninety miles of the driest country you ever wanted a drink in. And worse than the lack of water is the shale. What do you think it'll do to the camels? I've seen shod horses go lame in a day across that stretch. What do you think it'll do to unshod hoofs? Cut 'em to ribbons before you're one camp north of Beaver Lake. You won't have to worry about water. Jeff Davis won't have to worry about his camels. That shale will take care of. . . ."

"I don't want your opinions," snapped Travis.

"Not opinions," said Carnahan. "Facts."

"That will do!" Travis almost shouted. He stood there for a moment, fists clenched. Then he spoke with an effort. "I don't know why I even discussed it with you. It no longer concerns you. You're dismissed."

"But, sir. . . ."

"You're dismissed!" cried Travis. "Another word and I'll have you in irons!"

Face twisted like a whipped man's, Carnahan turned on his heel and walked stiffly out of the tent. He hadn't gone far when Maxeter followed him out of the lieutenant's quarters. The sergeant caught up with Carnahan, walking like a gorilla, his quick, catty steps tapping across the hard flats. His trousers were soiled with dirt and droppings and one puttee had come undone and was hanging sloppily about his shoe, and his sweat-darkened collar was unbuttoned around a thick red neck.

"How does it feel, Carnahan?" he said hoarsely. "How does it feel to crawl? I told you nobody made the clown of me."

"I must say you put your heart into your work," said Carnahan acidly. "It was you who told him about the girl?"

"The M.P. who stumbled across Pannah Parker's body in the Buckhorn was chasing a bunch out the back," said Maxeter. "He was sure one of them was a corporal from the Seventh, and there was a girl with this corporal. I always did think that Lidea Kerem had a high voice. Tie that together and you get the same squaw hitch I did."

"And you told Travis I found out about her at Indianola. You know that's a lie."

"Don't call me a liar, Carnahan," said Maxeter harshly. Then he relaxed, grinning. "The lieutenant really doesn't blame you for not telling him about the girl. Of course, it was the touch that ripped your stripes off, but, after all, such a pretty wench. . . ."

"How did he know about Dempewolff?" asked Carnahan.

"I told him," said Maxeter. "Dempewolff and Parker approached me in San Antonio with the same offer they gave you. I didn't make your mistake, Carnahan. I reported it to the lieutenant the minute he came back to camp."

Carnahan tried to reconcile that with his suspicions of Maxeter. If Maxeter had told Travis about Dempewolff that still didn't mean he wasn't working with Dempewolff. Yet, somehow, Carnahan hadn't looked for that much subtlety in Maxeter.

"But you told Travis the Devil's River country was safer than the route we'd planned," he said.

"I don't know where you got that idea," said Maxeter. "It was all the lieutenant's decision."

"And what decided him?" said Carnahan. "Your knowledge of the Devil's River? Too bad the native drivers had to get out of that riot alive, isn't it, Maxeter? If someone was trying to stop the camel experiment that way, they'll have to try all over again, won't they? Cutting the camels' hoofs to pieces on a rocky stretch, for instance. Do you favor the Devil's River route, Maxeter?"

Maxeter let go an explosive breath, and his body bent forward suddenly. Then he caught himself and stood that way, breathing heavily.

"No," he said. "No. I won't hit you, Carnahan. I won't give you that chance. The only one facing court-martial around here will be you. But you'll wish I *had* hit you before I'm through. You'll wish I'd put a bullet between your eyes like you did Parker. You'll wish you were as dead as Pannah Parker!"

V

I T was Carnahan's bunkmate who found the hand. Carnahan had left Maxeter and was going to his tent for his coat, because it would be chilly later on, and he was standing fatigue till twelve. He found Private Tatum in front of the Sibley, a bowlegged trooper with enough hash marks on his sleeve to account for more hitches in the cavalry than the rest of the troop put together. He held up a silver hand, gleaming softly in the moonlight.

"Found it hanging above the tent," he said, and his voice sounded strained.

Carnahan took the heavy piece of molded silver, studying it. He was about to speak when he remembered something. The hand of Fatima? He grinned suddenly, and hung the hand up again, tying its velvet string to the snap on the Sibley's flap.

"It's all right, Tatum," he told the frowning private. "Leave it there. I have an idea what it is."

The natives had pitched their tents in the greasewood beyond the camel lines. They were sitting cross-legged around a *mangal*—a copper brazier holding the glowing coals of their fire.

Hassan arose, bowing and touching his red fez and his lips and chest, with the tips of fat fingers. "*Salaam, effendi*," he said softly. "We hoped you would come."

The girl's face was no longer hidden by her burnoose. Her lustrous brown hair fell softly from beneath her velvet cap, framing the pale olive of her aquiline, infinitely aristocratic face. Her red lips were accentuated by the shadowed line of even white teeth that showed in her smile.

"You put that hand on my tent?" he asked her.

"To secure you from Sergeant Maxeter," she said. "I told you he has the Evil Eye. But you are protected now. Won't you join us?"

Carnahan sat cross-legged between the fat, chuckling Hassan and the girl, and was introduced to the drivers. The first wore a conical cap on his matted head and a naked dirk stuck through the twisted rope of velvet belting his white cotton robe, and his glittering eyes were filled with a wild fanaticism that reminded Carnahan of an Apache ready for the warpath.

"That is Rejeb," grinned Hassan. "He is a Mevlevi, a dancing dervish from the Tigris. You think your red men are fighters? *Inshallah!* You should see our Rejeb when he reaches his frenzy. From time immemorial, the dervishes have led the Moslem armies into battle. There is no warrior in the world more terrible."

There were two sullen Kurds from the camel bazaars of Damascus, with long *kurbashes* coiled at their belts, whips of cured goat hide tipped with sharp obsidian. And a bearded Yezeedi who mumbled to himself without seeming to hear the introduction. Jemel was the Arab who had been wounded the night before. Then Farrid Kerem, the girl's brother. He nodded his dark head gravely, fierce eyes meeting Carnahan's, voice hollow and ceremonious.

"*Nejerek sa'id unbarak,*" he said.

Carnahan looked helplessly at Hassan, and the fat little Turk grinned. "A saying from our country, *effendi*. Farrid is as full of sayings as a camel is of stomachs. Always mouthing them. He wishes that your day be blessed and happy."

Carnahan knew the Indian's love of oratory and cere-mony, and he sensed an affinity between these wild, for-eign tribesmen and the American Indians, and he spoke gravely, addressing himself to Farrid. "May your campfires still burn bright when the fires of your enemies are dead."

"Beard of the Prophet, your tongue is as smooth as Sal-adin's," laughed Hassan. He turned to Farrid, translating

96

what Carnahan had said, and Carnahan saw the momentary pleasure light Farrid's fierce eyes.

Hassan took out his inevitable *nargileh*, a long water pipe, and began puffing on it. "Farrid hasn't forgotten that you saved his life, *effendi*. Twice. Once there on the gangway at Indianola, when Sergeant Maxeter would have shot him. The drivers were not drunk in San Antonio for no true Moslem will touch liquor. But someone insulted the Prophet."

Farrid muttered something, and Carnahan turned to Hassan again. "What did he say?"

"Another one of our sayings," said Hassan. "There is no God but Allah, and Mohammed is his Prophet. It was how the fight started, you see. It is so easy to insult the Prophet. A wrong look, someone knocking off your fez. A Moslem will fight to the death over it. A Moslem feels strongly about his faith. And about his friends . . . Corporal, his *dostoums*. As I say, Farrid will never forget that you saved his life. He wishes you to have his sword. Legend says it is the blade of Saladin, handed down in Farrid's family from the time when Saladin showed Richard the Lion-Hearted that the steel that can part a silk scarf in mid-air is superior to the iron that hews an oak in two. It is from Damascus, the blade, and can be bent double without snapping."

Carnahan accepted the curved scimitar with its jewel-encrusted hilt, unable to speak for a moment, realizing what a tremendous honor it was. Hassan must have seen the flustered look on his face, for the Turk bent slightly toward him.

"To give a gift in return at this moment would insult him deeply, *effendi*. But a *tarbancha* . . ."—he glanced at Carnahan's Colt—"a revolver . . . is very near and dear to a warrior's heart, eh? Later, perhaps. By Allah, even I could put a *tarbancha* to profitable use. *Ai!*"

Carnahan grinned, then sobered, and turned to Farrid when he spoke. "Tell him that as long as the sword is in my hands, it shall never know dishonor."

Lidea Kerem translated to her brother this time, and, when she turned back, Carnahan asked her how she knew English.

"I am the daughter of Sheikh Mossul el Kerem," she said. "Our lands were in Syria, near the borders of Turkey. I was sent to England to be educated. On my return, I found my father's lands destroyed and my family dead but for Farrid. He had been wounded in the battle with the Arabs and had been saved by a servant, who took him to Smyrna. I found him there, tending camels for his living. When Major Wayne came and hired Farrid as a driver, I smuggled myself aboard the *Supply*. They wouldn't have taken a girl, but I managed to keep my sex secret till you discovered me the other night."

"You were in the lieutenant's tent, *effendi*," muttered Hassan. "Did you tell him?"

"About Lidea?" asked Carnahan. "He already knew. It was about something worse than that. Travis is changing our course to the Devil's River country. We'll have to cross a stretch of bad rock."

Hassan opened his mouth around his *nargileh*, throwing up fat hands in a Levantine gesture. "Nebuchadnezzar fray his beard! Doesn't he know that will ruin the camels? They've been months aboard the ship. Their hoofs are soft as yours. They'll be cut to bits on the rock."

"No way of shoeing them?"

Hassan shook his head. "No, *effendi*. We don't shoe our camels. Even if we did, how could we do it here? Why do you look so strange, *dostoum?*"

Carnahan was staring into the fire, and the dark, intense look narrowed his eyes. "No way of shoeing them? I think there is."

"But *dostoum*," said Hassan, "friend, we have no black-smith. . . ."

"Not iron," said Carnahan. "Another kind of shoes. The Indians were using it centuries before the Yankees hit Texas."

"How are you talking?" asked Hassan.

"The Mission Nuestra Señora de la Candelaria is the last civilized post between here and the Devil's River," said Carnahan. "They'll have what we need there. You'll see how I'm talking then, Hassan *dostoum*."

CARNAHAN finished fatigue at twelve, was relieved on the horse lines, and moved down through the darkness, past the heavy breathing of the weary stock, and the singular crunch of some camel still working his cud, and the silent row of conical Sibley tents. He was stopping to lift the flap of his own when a muffled grunt jerked him straight. He whirled around with his hand still holding the canvas.

In the darkness, all he caught was the dim hurtling form, the flash of an upraised gun, and its descent. Through the explosion of pain in his head, he heard his own sharp gasp. Then it was the hard ground beneath his back and the pain sweeping all sensation from him and the vague realization that the shadow above him was the man, striking again.

"Inshallah!"

The shout came from behind the shadowy figure, and, when the weight descended on him, Carnahan thought he had been struck again. But it was the man's body, with another struggling form on top of it. Breath knocked from him by the two falling bodies, Carnahan feebly tried to roll from beneath them.

"Damn you," gasped the man directly on top of him.

"Domus," panted the other. "Pig. . . ."

There was a sharp gasp. A boot caught Carnahan in the face. It was the first man scrambling to his feet and stumbling off into the darkness. The second one was still sprawled across Carnahan, and he felt how soft the body was suddenly, and looked up into the luminous eyes of Lidea Kerem. She smiled and rose to her knees, holding up a short knife, tipped with a dark stain.

"I drew the pig's blood," she breathed heavily.

Tatum had shoved a sleepy head out of the flap, asking what the hell was the matter, and the guard was running down past the row of Sibleys, and the two men in the next tent were outside in their underwear, but all Carnahan was aware of was the girl.

"He would have killed me."

Lidea Kerem nodded. "I've been waiting for it. I saw him follow you from the camel lines. I told you that Maxeter had the Evil Eye."

His glance went up past her face to something hanging from the flap of the tent directly above his head and gleaming softly in the darkness. It was the hand of Fatima.

VI

CARNAHAN heard the sudden, raucous screaming, and turned his mount in time to see Private Mullaney fall off his rearing camel.

"*Hyah!*" Carnahan called to his own camel. "*Hyah. Hoosh.*"

The lumbering *djemel-mai* paced back toward the fallen man. They were in the incredibly dry, desolate badlands of the Devil's River, with the camp at Frío Cañon four days behind them. Lieutenant Travis had begun putting his cavalrymen on the camels, but the men were resentful and suspicious of the strange beasts. There were only three of the single-humped racing Thoroughbreds in the train, and they belonged to the tribesmen, and the troopers had to ride the immense, double-humped *djemel-mais* from Farther Asia, ponderous, plodding draft animals with a spine-jolting gait and a vicious temper.

Carnahan had always been a consummate horseman, and Farrid and Lidea had taught him enough so that he could maintain a comparatively easy seat. But he was the only one who had befriended the natives, and an enmity existed between Farrid and the rest of the Americans that prevented much co-operation.

"Damn' thing balked, and, when I tried to kick it ahead, it turned and bit me," snarled Mullaney.

"Do you kick your horse ahead?" said Carnahan.

"No, but these ain't horses. . . ."

"You'll never stay on these camels till you learn they aren't much different from horses," said Carnahan, and anger had crept into his voice. "It takes patience. Kicking 'em won't do any good. You can make most vicious horses halfway gentle if you treat them right long enough. Try giving him some slack in your rein when he balks. Maybe you're pulling him in."

Sergeant Maxeter could afford to be laughing as he rode up because he was forking a horse, and none of his mule-skinners had to put up with the camels. Hassan had caught the runaway *djemel-mai* and was leading it back as Lieutenant Travis galloped toward them from the head of the caravan, dust on his gray turned to a thick cake by drying lather.

"You having trouble again, Mullaney?" he said angrily. "I thought you were a cavalryman."

"*Barrak*, you son of a dog," Hassan told the camel. "*Barrak*."

"Hold it, Turkey!" Maxeter shouted at him, and swung down off his horse, moving in toward the camel. "Maybe this is what the trouble's all about. What's that on his feet?"

Travis swung his gray in closer and stepped off, bending to look. The camel's hoofs were encased in queer-looking sacks of thick rawhide, pulled tightly around the cannon bone with a drawstring. Still bent over, Travis looked at Carnahan.

"What is it, Private?"

"Shoes," said Carnahan. "Indian shoes. The Comanches used to protect their horse's hoofs that way before they knew about iron. Barefoot, those camels would have been finished the first day. You can see what the shale has done to that rawhide already, and you know it's as tough as iron."

The baffled expression on Maxeter's face gave Carnahan an intense satisfaction. "I wondered. . . ."

"Why the camels didn't go lame?" grinned Carnahan. "I thought you would begin to pretty soon. When we stopped at the Señora Mission, the girl got rawhide from the *padre* there."

"Seems to me you're taking a lot into your own hands, Private," said Travis. He stood there a moment, watching Carnahan, and there was a strange speculation in his eyes. Finally he let out a heavy breath. "Don't go too far, Carnahan, that's all, just don't go too far. You haven't got room for another slip. We'll pitch camp on those flats ahead now. . . ."

He turned to swing aboard his gray, and the chin chains on his government bit made a sharp rattle as he jerked the horse around and booted it into a gallop. Through bitter experience, Maxeter's 'skinners had learned to pitch the horse lines at a safe distance to the windward of the camel lines, and Carnahan was beginning to unsaddle his *djemel-mai* when he heard the man coming up the line.

> Oh, I'd like to be a packer, and pack
> with George F. Crook,
> And dressed up in my canvas suit. . . .

Sergeant Maxeter stopped singing as he came up behind Carnahan, and for a moment the heavy breathing was the only sound. Carnahan pulled the hump bridle off his camel. It had been a maddening day with the troopers fighting the camels all the way, and Carnahan hoped that Maxeter wouldn't ride him too hard now because he could feel himself knotting up already.

"Clever little trick of yours, putting buckskin boots on

those camels," said Maxeter. "I guess you think you're pretty smart."

Carnahan's fingers closed around the hump till they showed white at the knuckles. He was hot and sweaty and the alkali covered his clothes and grated against his skin and tasted, bitter and acrid, in his mouth. *Just take it easy*, he told himself, *just take it easy*.

"The girl got the buckskin from the *padre?*" said Maxeter. "I guess she thinks she's pretty smart, too. You and she get along pretty well, don't you?"

Carnahan turned to the girth. "Let's not talk about her."

"Oh," said Maxeter, and laughed harshly. "I see. Who'd ever thought Private Eddie Carnahan would go sweet on a damned native woman."

"Shut up."

Carnahan stopped himself there, standing rigidly where he had turned to face the sergeant. His chest rose and fell with the angry breath passing through him. *Take it easy.* He licked his lips. *Take it easy.* Maxeter began shifting to the side.

"Don't get too close to the camel, Sergeant."

"Sweet on a damn' desert wench," grinned Maxeter. "That's worse than being a squaw man."

Carnahan's words came out through his teeth. "You make a mistake thinking of her that way. Native woman? Her people were civilized before your ancestors came down out of the trees. Ever hear of the Assyrians? Nineveh? Tyre? The Tigris was the center of the civilized world four thousand years ago. It would take you that long to reach the refinement she has, and then I don't think you'd make it. Don't get too close to the camel, Sergeant."

"Refinement?" Maxeter laughed. "She isn't any more refined than an Indian squaw, and you know it."

"Sergeant, the camel. . . ."

But it was too late. The *djemel-mai* had been leaning over on one side, and the weight was off his hind leg now, and the hoof came up with a swinging circular motion that caught Maxeter right where he sat his McClellan.

Breath exploding from him in an agonized gasp, Maxeter hurtled forward onto his face, digging a furrow with his nose through the shale. He stopped sliding, and rolled over and jumped to his feet, shaking his head dazedly, pawing blood from his face. The bitter curses erupted from him like hot vitriol. He looked from side to side, saw what he wanted, and scooped up one of the heavy picket pins lying beside the camel lines.

"I'll show that knock-kneed, hare-lipped, cross-eyed son of a calico mule . . . ," he brayed, jumping at the camel with the picket pin upraised.

Carnahan threw himself between the sergeant and the *djemel-mai*, lean body crashing across Maxeter's knees. They both rolled to the ground, and Carnahan scrambled off the non-com's legs, jumping erect.

"I've been working that camel four days now," he panted. "Nobody does that to my animal, horse or camel!"

Still gripping the pin, Maxeter got to his feet. His pig eyes were mere slits, and his thick neck was swelled with rage.

"And nobody does that to me," he said apoplectically. "I'd kill the mule that kicked me. I'd kill the man that knocked me down. This has been coming too long, Carnahan!"

Carnahan tried to duck aside, but the pin caught him on the shoulder, and he went down sideways with the pain shooting through his right side and blinding him to anything else for a moment. He was on the ground then, with the sergeant straddling him and beating at his head. Carnahan rolled over, throwing up his arms to cover his head, and tried to rise. Maxeter's gorilla body was heavy on him, and the pin smashed down on his arm, and he thought it was broken.

With a final desperation, he tore his arms from above his head and put his hands flat on the ground, and on his hands and knees like that, heaved upward. Maxeter rode him like a bucking broncho, beating at his head with the pin, screaming and cursing in his rage.

Carnahan's head jerked down to the first blow, but his body kept on coming up. He jerked to the second blow, and heard his own gasp of pain. Then he was on his feet, whirling to clutch the pin as Maxeter jumped back to keep from falling. Carnahan caught the man's wrist, and they came together and swayed there. Maxeter tore his thick wrist free, and struck with the pin. Carnahan took the blow, clinging to the sweaty, writhing body in his grasp.

"Carnahan!" someone was shouting, and he heard the pound of feet behind him. "Carnahan, as you were . . . !"

But Maxeter shifted to strike again. Desperately Carnahan drove a fist into the sergeant's belly. Maxeter only grunted, and the pin came down. Carnahan slid halfway down the sergeant's body, still keeping his arm around Maxeter's waist. He snaked a lean leg behind Maxeter's knee. Maxeter grunted as he brought the pin down again.

Sobbing, Carnahan threw his weight against the non-com. His body carried Maxeter backward. Then the sergeant tripped over that leg behind him, and went down, and Car-

106

nahan followed him like that, smashing a fist into his face.

Carnahan stumbled over the sergeant's body, and whirled back before Maxeter could rise. The sergeant tried to roll away, but Carnahan grabbed him by the collar and stepped across him. Standing above Maxeter, astraddle him, Carnahan pulled him upwards and hit him brutally in the face. Maxeter gasped and tried to jerk free.

"No," sobbed Carnahan in a strangled, desperate way, and pulled him straight again and up off the ground, and hit him in the face.

The sergeant slammed against the ground beneath the blow, and his gasp of pain hardly sounded human. Carnahan pulled him up and knocked him back again. Maxeter's body stiffened. Again Maxeter made that garbled, animal sound of pain, pawing one hand up to grab feebly at Carnahan. Carnahan drew his fist back, face twisted with the blind rage sweeping him.

Someone caught his fist from behind.

He tried to jerk free, any sane thought blotted out by his savage desire to smash Maxeter once and for all. Then someone else was on him, and someone else, and he was jerking and cursing and fighting the weight of bodies bearing him down. They got his arms twisted around behind him, and he was helpless in their grasp.

They dragged him off Maxeter. Lieutenant Travis swam into Carnahan's spinning vision. The young officer was white with rage. He wouldn't trust himself to speak for a moment. Finally he made a hasty gesture with one hand.

"Get some water for this man. Hear me? Get some water."

The muleskinners were gathered in a bunch on one side, separated from the cavalrymen who had come up from the horse lines. A 'skinner got a canteen and dumped a little of the precious water into Maxeter's face, slapping him. The sergeant groaned. Finally he rolled over and tried to get to his feet, and failed. The 'skinner helped him sit up. Maxeter sat there a moment, pawing at his bloody face, drawing his breath in with small, sobbing sounds.

"I could have you both for this," said Travis thinly.

"Defending m'self," mumbled the sergeant, through smashed lips. "Attacked me. "What c'd I do? Defending m'self. . . ."

"I thought as much," said Travis, turning to Carnahan. "This is the last, Carnahan. I'm putting you in irons. I won't even bother with a summary. You'll have a full court-martial when we reach Santa Fé. You'll get the firing squad, Carnahan!"

VII

FROM earliest times, the Jornada del Muerto had been dreaded by all travelers coming up into New Mexico from the south. The Devil's River country had been a picnic compared with this Journey of the Dead, stretching eastward from the Río Grande for ninety miles, an incredible desolation, utterly devoid of water, barren of life but for a few, scuttling vinegaroons, rock-ribbed hills and sandy wastes spotted with meager clumps of sere dry soap weed, or mesquite that could hardly pass for vegetation.

As he sat dully in the fetid oppression beneath the dusty canvas tilt of the ambulance that had been his prison for the past week, Private Carnahan's wrist irons rattled dismally as he reached up to pull at a sweat-soaked collar. He licked dry, cracked lips and looked impatiently out the puckered rear of the hood. Why didn't they bring his water? Reveille roll call was over, and the sounds of breakfast came dimly to him through the dawning day. He wasn't hungry, but he wished Tatum would hurry up with his water.

He raised his head toward the end of the wagon. "Tatum?"

It wasn't Tatum. It was a pair of cavalrymen in full uniform, and they unhitched the tailgate and let it down. Lieutenant Travis stood farther out.

"All right," one of them said.

Carnahan crawled out and slid down the tailgate. An ominous quiet hung over the camp. A squad of muleskinners shifted nervously around a kneeling *djemel-mai*. In their midst, Carnahan could see the litters of its pack saddle still on the ground, and the skin containers in which the water was carried, looking oddly flat. Face pale and set, Travis moved in and lifted Carnahan's hands, rattling the chain on the irons, yanking at the manacles. Then he turned to one of the cavalrymen. The trooper stiffened.

"He couldn't have gotten out without me seeing him, sir," said the soldier. "My post was directly behind the ambulance. I relieved Private Tatum at twelve."

"What's the matter?" asked Carnahan.

"Somebody," said Travis, "put a knife in the water containers. Slit every single one. The only water we have left is in the canteens. That won't last us the day."

Hassan came over from where the muleskinners stood about one of the emptied water containers and shoved his little red fez back on his fat head, grinning. "Whoever thought they could stop us by doing that to the water bags didn't know much about camels, *effendi*."

Travis turned sharply. "What do you mean?"

"*Ai*, you don't know, either?" said Hassan. "Haven't you heard how the *oont* can travel without water?"

A strained look crossed Travis's face. "You've proved that story false yourself. You've watered the beasts every day. Twenty gallons or more. You told me yourself."

"That was when we had water." Hassan smiled. "Of course, we water them whenever we can. But when a camel is *gizu*, it can go almost a week without drinking."

"*Gizu?*"

Hassan nodded blandly. "Capable of living off herbage alone, without needing water. These animals have been well-watered along the route, and they are certainly *gizu* now."

Travis spoke tightly. "What does that get us? We have no water for the horses and mules, or the men. This isn't ordinary country, where a man can stay alive five or six days without water. Without any liquid to replace what that sun evaporates, you'll literally dry up within two or three days. And we've got a week's march before we get out of the Jornada, even pushing the animals to the utmost."

Hassan was smiling secretively. "But we have liquid, *effendi*."

Travis bent forward, and Carnahan saw the white band of flesh appear around his compressed lips. "What are you talking about?"

"As I say, *effendi*," said Hassan, "whoever slit the water bags certainly didn't know anything about camels. Among the *djemel-mais* are seven cows, and they are still in milk. That is enough liquid to last your horses and mules and men a day or so."

"Only prolonging the end," said Travis with a heavy breath.

"No," said Hassan. "After the milk, there is the camel's bladder. You said we have watered the camels every day? *Ai, effendi*. Twenty gallons. And when we have milked the cows dry, we begin killing them and getting the green water from their bladders. It is another expedience we utilize in the Syrian deserts. And even doing it that way, we should be able to reach the end of the Jornada without having to kill too many of *Effendi* Davis's pets, eh? Twenty gallons to the camel will take us a long way, on short rations."

Travis stood without speaking, and Carnahan tried to fathom the strange look on his face, and couldn't. A horse snorted from down the line somewhere; the troopers shifted uneasily in the sand. Finally the lieutenant forced a smile.

"Well," he said huskily, "well, it looks as if we'll get through, after all, doesn't it? Thank you, Hassan. Yes, thank you."

He turned and walked stiffly around the ambulance, that strangely taut look still on his pale face. Carnahan didn't blame him much; the sudden relief from thinking they were going to die like that left him feeling shaky himself. He climbed back into the ambulance, and soon the wagon jolted and rattled, and sand began its greedy suck at the rolling wheels.

THAT night the girl brought Carnahan his supper of biscuits and jerky, and a canteen full of camel's milk. It was foul, sour, hot stuff, but Carnahan gulped it greedily. Then he became aware of the girl studying him, and he turned toward her, realizing that she had filled the fetid interior of the ambulance with a faint, ineffable perfume. He licked his lips.

"I thought all your women went veiled," he said, to hide his growing embarrassment.

She smiled softly, still watching him in that intent way. "In our country, perhaps. Farrid wanted me to go veiled here, but I told him we were in a new country, and should do as you do. Would you want me to wear a veil?"

"No," he said sharply. "It wouldn't be right to hide such a beautiful . . . ," he stumbled, flustered. "What I mean is. . . ."

"I think I know what you mean." She laughed mischievously, and then sobered. "But this isn't a time to talk like that, is it? I came in to ask you about the Indians. The soldiers mentioned them."

He nodded. "This part of the New Mexico has always been dangerous. All year 'round some Apaches are riding war horses on the Camino Real or down from the Staked Plains. But I have a hunch we don't have to worry about a chance raid so much."

"I don't understand."

"Whoever slit the water bags," said Carnahan, "undoubtedly kept out enough water for himself to reach safety. Where it will take the caravan a week, a man riding a fast horse could get out of the Jornada in two days. The same holds true on the trip between here and San Antone. A man riding a horse could have pushed past us long ago. Carl Dempewolff, for instance. For all the traveling he does as an agent for Harris Shippers, it's always seemed to me that Dempewolff had less trouble with Indians than a man should. It's been rumored up at Bowie that he has some suspicious connections with more than one of the tribes. I think it's about time he was using his connections. I think these attempts to stop us so far have been little flurries. I think it's about time for the big blow."

"You say *whoever*," she muttered impatiently. "You know who slit the water bags as well as I. . . ." She stopped as someone came up the line singing, passed the wagon, and went on by, with the song dying away finally.

> Oh, I'd like to be a packer, and pack with
> George F. Crook
> And dressed up in my canvas suit, I'd be
> for him mistook. . . .

THE carcasses of half a dozen *djemel-mais*, killed for their water, lay rotting behind the weary caravan as it pulled out of the desolate Jornada into the mesa country, marking the approach to the Río Grande. The scouts began to find Indian sign now, and Carnahan had taken to sitting up front with Tatum, a dark, waiting look to his eyes.

It was after a noon halt that they rose out of a sink and topped a sandstone ridge, and Tatum spat his tobacco juice disgustedly. "Damn. Travis could've hunted a million years without finding a better way to skylight us. What's wrong with him? There was some jack timber half a mile to the left. You could see it from the bottoms. Taken us through that over the top and we would've been screened some decent, anyway."

Travis had mounted Corporal O'Malley, of Maxeter's 'skinners, and the rattle of his accouterments preceded him from behind the wagon. Tatum shifted his quid to a cheek and pointed toward a notch in the line of mesas ahead. "Travis ain't heading toward there?"

Corporal O'Malley shoved a forage cap back on curly red hair. "That's his orders. He took Maxeter out on patrol an hour ago and left command to head through that notch."

"Out on patrol?" said Tatum. "You must be mistaken. Not even Travis would be fool enough to take his only top-kick and leave this whole caravan in the hands of a non-com."

"He did," said O'Malley, flushing.

"That notch is the sweetest spot for an ambush an Apache ever shook his eagle feather at," said Carnahan. "Look at the timber coming down either slope right up to the trail. You can't take us through there, O'Malley."

The red-headed 'skinner stiffened. "That's my orders, Carnahan. I'm throwing out flankers to take care of the timber."

"Flankers!" Carnahan stood up in the seat of the jolting wagon, face darkening. "You couldn't take care of that timber with a whole corps. And how about your advance?"

"Travis is taking care of the forward scouting," said O'Malley.

"And with your flankers gone, how many men does that leave guarding the caravan?" asked Carnahan hotly. "This is crazy, O'Malley. You can't take us through the notch. There's open country around the south end of those mesas where we can at least see what's coming. You won't have to weaken us by sending out so many men."

O'Malley's voice was brittle. "I've got my orders."

"Then I'm changing them!" roared Carnahan. "You're heading around the south end. I order you. . . ."

"*You* order me?" O'Malley rose in his stirrups. Then he

sat down again, laughing contemptuously. "Officers' School gave you a big head, didn't it, Private Carnahan? You aren't in any position to order me, now or ever. I'm heading through the notch."

He trotted on toward the front, riding tightly in the saddle as all Army men did. Carnahan stood there a moment on the swaying, rattling footboards of the box seat, fists clenched in his manacles. Then he sat down again, muttering sullenly.

They were well into the notch when Tatum half stood, swearing, and then dropped back down, hauling his mules to a halt. The man who came staggering out of the trees wasn't an Indian. The front of his blue coat was bloody, and he held his hands gripped across his belly as if to keep the life in him that way, and he weaved across the trail with his head down and bumped up against the ambulance, and turned around and sat down with his back against the front wheel. By that time, Carnahan had jumped off the seat and was standing over Sergeant Maxeter.

"Travis," gasped the sergeant, still holding his belly with his hammy hands. "Travis, all along. He got the patrol up in one of those coulées on the other slope, said he'd scout the ridge hisself before we topped it. Soon's he was gone, they came down on us. Mescalero Apaches. I took it in my belly and fell beneath my horse. Those mescal-eaters must've thought I was dead. When it was over, Travis came back. With Dempewolff. . . ."

"Lieutenant Travis," said Carnahan hollowly. "And all the time I thought it was you."

"And I thought it was you," panted Maxeter weakly. "Guess Dempewolff went to Travis as a last resort after missing fire on you and me. It would've been easy enough for Dempewolff to push past us by way of El Paso and make a deal with those mescal-eaters after Travis slipped up on the water bags. Soon's they left the coulée, I wiggled from under my horse and made for you. They're right behind me, Carnahan. . . ."

"We didn't see who tried to put my lights out back at Frío Cañon, but we thought it was you there, too," said Carnahan. "Travis? Why?"

"Saw you getting chummy with Farrid, I guess," said Maxeter. "Maybe he didn't want it to get any further. Figured you and the natives might cook up something to botch his little idea of cutting the camel's hoofs up. Which you did. I told you the Devil's River route was his idea."

"But it was you who took the camel drivers into San Antone. . . ."

"Hell, yes!" Maxeter strangled, spit blood. "And I'd do it again. I'm a muleskinner, see. I thought it would fix things to get those natives drunk, but they wouldn't touch the stuff. I'd left 'em before the trouble started. I'm a mule-skinner, see, and the quicker I get shuck of this crazy detail, the better. Didn't figure on getting shuck this way, though, did I . . . ?" He laughed crazily, gasped.

Already Tatum was running up the line of march, yelling the alarm, and the natives were halting the camels and pulling them into the hollow square they called a *zarriba*. Maxeter pawed at Carnahan with a callused hand.

"That girl, though," he choked. "Lidea Kerem. I was wrong about her, Carnahan. She ain't no native wench. She's as white as the girl I left behind at Circle City, see. Nineveh? That what you said? Assyria? Sure. Refined?

Sure. You get hitched with her, Carnahan. I'm telling you. I saw how she acted on this trip. Not a whimper. All through the Jornada. Took it better'n the men. Make a fine wife for a young lieutenant. And you'll be a Mister, Carnahan. Get these camels through and they'll send you to the Academy double-time. I wouldn't be surprised if Jeff Davis himself put through the recommendation. . . ."

He grinned suddenly, and slumped back against the wheel. His hands relaxed against his belly.

> Oh, I'd like to be a packer, and pack
> with George . . . F. . . . Crook. . . .

His voice trailed off as he fell sideways from the wheel. "Carnahan," shouted O'Malley, racing by on his horse. "Get back in that ambulance. They're coming!"

VIII

THE sound of camels and mules and shouting drivers had risen to an insane bedlam now. A 'skinner ran from between the ambulance and the next wagon, and flopped to one knee suddenly, Springfield coming to position, and bellowing. Then a little round hole appeared in his forehead, and he dropped the rifle and fell forward on his face.

The Mescalero Apaches were flooding out of the dark timber on a horde of calico ponies that shook the ground with their thunder. There was a big Roman-nosed Indian leading them, with gold earrings in his lobes and a red bandanna around his black head and a Sam Colt Paterson in each hand. That was about all Carnahan had time to see.

He tried to scoop up the dead 'skinner's Springfield, but it was a muzzleloader, and his hands were manacled on too short a chain for that. He dropped the rifle and sprinted on past the kicking spans of mules hauling the Murphy directly behind the ambulance. It was the wagon in which they had loaded his gear. As he swung up over the tailgate, Hassan lurched by, tugging a camel.

"Give me a *tarbancha!*" shouted the fat little Turk. "Oh, won't somebody please give me a *tarbancha.*"

Carnahan found his saddlebags in the wagon just behind the front seat. He was fumbling through them for his revolver when the Murphy shuddered from a violent impact outside. He saw the driver heave up in the front seat, struggling with a naked Mescalero. Face twisted fiendishly, the Apache raised his Bowie knife. The driver fell back in the bed with the blade in him up to the hilt, and the Mescalero followed him. Carnahan hadn't found his Colt yet, and he caught the glitter of steel as he whirled to meet the Apache.

He put a shoulder into the Indian and bent and rolled him over his back, and was bent over still when he whipped the sword from beneath his saddlebags. He jerked around with the curved scimitar Farrid had given him held in both hands. The Apache was just rising, and he screamed with the steel going into him.

The wagon shuddered again as a hidden horse smashed into it from outside, and with the sword bloody in his hands Carnahan dropped out of the burning wagon into the madness of charging, whirling horses and running troopers and bellowing guns.

The Indians were everywhere, racing through the scattered caravan in ones and twos and larger bunches. Hassan waddled by after a runaway *djemel-mai*.

"Give me a *tarbancha*, oh, somebody give me a *tarbancha . . . !*"

Farther back, Corporal O'Malley had formed a squad of riflemen, and their steady fire had cleared a little space around them. Carnahan dodged aside suddenly as a hurtling shape bore down on him. Then he stopped, staring wildly.

"*Barrak*, you son-of-a-djinn, *barrak!*" shouted the girl, as she hauled her dromedary to a halt.

The camel with her jerked to his fore knees, then folded its hind legs, and was kneeling beside Carnahan. Lidea Kerem's own mount wheeled uncontrollably, and she turned in the saddle to shout at Carnahan. "Jemel's *hejin*," she yelled, flinging a hand at the kneeling mount. "Take it, quick. Jemel won't need it any more."

Carnahan was already in the saddle, his voice rising above the din. "*Goom*, you son-of-a-*djinn, goom.*"

The fawn-colored racing dromedary heaved to its feet, and Carnahan whirled it to follow the girl. A Mescalero came pounding through the mêlée and almost struck the camel. Rearing his calico pony, the Indian jerked up an old Sharps muzzleloader, firing point-blank at the *hejin*.

Carnahan felt the camel jerk to the .50 caliber slug. Instinctively he freed himself from the saddle to jump when the beast went down. Then he jammed his legs against the side and bent over on the hump suddenly, because he remembered what Hassan had told him. The *hejin* kept right on running, and Carnahan saw the amazed look on the Apache's face as he raced by.

When he reached the riflemen, Carnahan pirouetted his camel with a skillful tug on the reins, voice hoarse. "Get yourselves a camel and form over by those Murphys."

O'Malley rose, bloody and smudged with powder smoke, waving his Colt. "You aren't giving orders here, Carnahan. You're a prisoner."

But three or four of the men wore the canary-yellow stripe of the cavalry down their pants legs, and Carnahan had commanded them when he wore his corporal's chevrons, and he yelled at them. "Get yourselves a camel, damn you. These are my men, O'Malley, and I'm mounting them. You can't do anything here."

A bunch of howling Apaches thundered by in a cloud of their own dust, hanging on the offside of their horses and firing over the animal's backs. A muleskinner fell across O'Malley's feet. Several of the cavalrymen had already started after their camels.

Hassan waddled by, waving a Colt six-shooter in his fat hands. "I've got a *tarbancha!*" he shouted, laughing like a child with a new toy.

Three Mescaleros charged out of the smoke in front of the Turk. Hassan kept right on going forward in his duck-footed jog-trot, lowered the gun, and fired. The first Indian pitched from his bare horse with a scream.

"*Tarbancha*," chortled Hassan, and fired again, and the second Indian tumbled off his mount. He fired again, and the third one slid down from his animal as it went past Hassan and fell on the Turk and carried him to the ground. But Hassan was on his feet again when Carnahan raced by, heading to round up a running camel.

The girl was beside Carnahan when they passed the native drivers. Farrid had managed to picket a half dozen *djemel-màis* in a *zarriba*, and he and the two wild Kurds and several Arabs were firing over their backs with Springfields taken from dead troopers. The girl leaned off her *hejin*, shouting at her brother. Farrid began yelling orders to his Kurds and the camels.

"*Goom, goom . . . !*"

By the time Carnahan had caught a camel and led it back to where his troopers were, Farrid and his men were there with the girl, astride plunging, rearing *djemel-mais*. Carnahan rose up in his saddle, lifting the gleaming scimitar in manacled hands.

"Left front into line . . . gallop!"

The half dozen troopers obeyed in a ragged fashion, fighting their camels in behind Carnahan, and, although the natives didn't understand the order, they followed the soldiers. Carnahan urged his *hejin* into a gallop with his weird squadron following him in a screaming, shouting bunch. He led them around the burning wagons and down the line of scattered camels and mules. A big bunch of Apaches was circling O'Malley and his 'skinners, and Carnahan struck them almost before they saw him coming, the huge lumbering camels towering over the small Indian ponies by half the height of a man. Carnahan leaned from his saddle, his sword made a gleaming arc in the air, and he saw the blood redden the Apache's bronze hide before the man went off his horse.

The Roman-nosed Mescalero swept into Carnahan, both his Patersons blazing as fast as he could thumb the hammers. Carnahan felt the camel jerk spasmodically to each slug, but he knew how it was now, and, riding with his tight Army seat and his fiendish grin, he reined the *hejin* over into the pinto, swinging the scimitar at the turkey-red bandanna on the Mescalero's black head.

The Patersons flamed in his face, blinding him, deafening him, and he felt a slug twitch off his forage cap and clip flesh from his ear, and a numbing impact drove his leg against the hairy side of the camel. Then his sword had finished its arc, and the Roman-nosed Apache dropped both his Patersons as he went off his horse.

Too filled with the wild red haze of battle to feel whatever wounds he had, Carnahan swung his *hejin* around, crashing into the rumps of two Indian ponies and unhorsing both riders as he pounded between them.

Rejeb, the dancing dervish, careened out of the smoke on a wild-eyed *djemel-mai*, smashing into a racing Apache. The Indian jumped at him, and they both went off the camel and rolled into the dust. The Indian rose first, but Rejeb bounced off the ground at him with his gleaming dirk, and the Apache took the steel with a howl that had no sound in the deafening roar of battle. Rejeb's yells were soundless, too, but Carnahan could make the words out by the movement of his lips.

"*Inshallah!*" he screamed, and turned to charge madly at a bunch of whirling horses. "*Mohammetallah . . . !*"

What had Hassan said? *You should see our Rejeb when he reaches his frenzy.* Carnahan understood what he meant now. The dancing dervish threw himself bodily at the first charging Indian, slamming up against the pinto and catching the Apache about the waist, and stabbing with the knife. He staggered away from the horse and had to run madly to keep from falling with his own momentum, and the Apache was reeling in his buffalo saddle with his stomach spurting blood.

Some of the Mescaleros were armed with short bows, and the first feathered shaft did no more than jerk Rejeb as it drove through his skinny chest. Carnahan could see the froth whitening the dancing dervish's mouth. The second arrow caused him to stagger, but he kept on going forward, butting head first into another horse. Whirled around by the impact, he swung wildly with his reddened blade, ripping the Indian's arm from wrist to shoulder. Rejeb caught himself from falling and turned again toward the Apache with the short bow, and with the first two shafts sticking out of him, front and rear, stumbled onward, screaming.

The third shaft took him in the belly. He bent double, and staggered on in a zigzag run. *You should see our Rejeb when he reaches his frenzy.* He was still going forward when he lurched into the rearing horse ridden by the Apache with the bow. The Indian twisted in his saddle, bowstring drawn to his ear with the fourth arrow notched.

"*Inshallah!*" shouted Rejeb, and, with the fourth shaft driving into him, clawed up on the horse and drove his knife into the Indian's chest, and the Indian fell off onto Rejeb, and they disappeared together in the billowing clouds of dust.

Farrid charged by with one of his bearded Kurds. A trio of Indians quartered into them, firing madly, and went on by with the surprise stamped into their faces as the camels didn't go down. The Kurd wheeled his *djemel-mai* after the last Indian, and his long *karbush* lashed out. The whip curled around and around the Apache's waist and pulled him off his pinto.

Everywhere Carnahan turned now, he saw that frustrated surprise in the Indians as their bullets failed to down the camels. And the surprise was turning to fear, because it was something beyond the Apaches' comprehension. Several of Carnahan's troopers had been shot from their saddles, but no matter how much lead the Indians poured into the camels themselves, the lumbering beasts wouldn't fall.

That finished it.

Unable to face these strange animals that refused to die and the crazed fiends who rode them, the Apaches broke and scattered up the slope. One of their leaders tried to re-form them, but Carnahan led his squadron on up and smashed into the handful of horsemen gathering in the trees. He was plunging through the timber like that when he caught the movement on the ridge above and a gleam of metal that could have come from military accouterments.

The Indians were done, and, leaving Farrid to clean it up, Carnahan pulled his *hejin* away from the scattering Indians and forced it into a run up the slope. He topped the ridge going full tilt, and saw them ahead of him, just galloping off on the other slope onto the flats beyond.

They must have waited there on the ridge to see the finish of the caravan, Lieutenant Travis and Carl Dempewolff, and now they caught Carnahan as he was skylighted going over the top, and their horses suddenly picked up speed. But Carnahan plunged down the slope, reached the flats, and rapidly closed the intervening space, his *hejin* covering the ground in that padding gait. The first shot stabbed redly into the dusk, and the whine of lead swept past Carnahan. Bent low in the saddle, he raced on forward into them.

"Carnahan!" shouted Dempewolff, in a squawking, choked way, emptying his six-gun wildly at the crazy figure towering above him.

Saladin's sword gleamed in the dusk as Carnahan swung it upward. Dempewolff screamed, pulling to one side, the twisted fear dimly apparent on the white blot of his face. The curved blade swept past him, but he had gone too far over, and his foot snapped from the stirrup. He went off and hit on his neck, and his body was a still, dead shadow on the dark ground passing behind Carnahan.

Haughty and bitter and proud, Lieutenant Travis had turned his long-legged gray and was rushing back down on Carnahan with his cavalry saber out. They met with a shock that almost unseated Carnahan. His weight was thrown for a moment on his off leg, and it collapsed beneath him, and only then did he remember the bullet he had taken through it. He caught wildly at the pommel of his saddle, almost dropping the scimitar.

Standing in the stirrups of his wheeling horse, Travis was as high as Carnahan. He gasped something, hacking at Carnahan with his deadly saber. Carnahan couldn't help his scream of agony as the steel bit into his shoulder. He twisted around, able only to thrust with the point of his blade. Jerking his gray broadside, Travis hacked again. Carnahan parried, steel ringing on steel.

"Damn' dog-robber . . . !" panted Travis, and he jerked up in his stirrups again and struck down.

Carnahan caught the blow with his scimitar, but was driven forward against his saddle by the stunning force of it. Lying across his plunging *hejin*, he saw the gleaming steel flash down.

With a fast, desperate curse, he threw himself bodily out of leather, smashing into Travis. His lean body carried the lieutenant off the other side of the gray, and, as they fell, Carnahan thrust hard with Saladin's blade and heard Travis scream.

Carnahan didn't know how long he lay across the body of Lieutenant Travis, weak and dizzy from loss of blood and utterly exhausted from the violent battle and the long ride, and filled with sick pain from his wounds. He was dimly conscious of night falling like a thick, black curtain over him, and then the stars coming out, and finally the shadowy forms padding up and blotting out the stars. It was Lidea Kerem and that faint perfume of hers, and the silky sense of her hair falling across his face as she bent over him.

"Beard of Allah," chortled Hassan. "He isn't hurt very much if he can grin like that."

Carnahan made a faint gesture with his hand. "This is a crazy place to say it, I guess, but I'm going to ask you before I go. I wanted to ask you in the wagon, but I couldn't somehow. What I mean is, maybe a corporal isn't so much, or a private, now, but it's as Maxeter said, when I prove Travis was the one, his ripping off my stripes won't count, and, if I get the camels through, Army life isn't so bad, if you get a halfway decent post like Bowie. What I mean is, there are lots of women in Brass Buttons Row there. . . ."

"I know what you mean," she said softly, "but in my country it is a custom for a man to ask a girl's family about things like that."

Perhaps Farrid couldn't understand English, but what

they had been talking about must have been made plain enough to him by the look in their eyes, because, when Carnahan turned to him, Farrid spoke before Carnahan could say anything, a grin splitting his dark, fierce face for a moment.

"You'll have to translate," said Carnahan.

"Just another of Farrid's sayings," chuckled Hassan. "He is always mouthing them. Farrid said . . . 'He who does not invite me to his wedding will not have me at his funeral.'"

THE STING OF SEÑORITA SCORPION

Les Savage, Jr., narrated the adventures of Elgera Douglas, better known as *Señorita* Scorpion, in a series of seven short novels that originally appeared in *Action Stories*, published by Fiction House. She was, by far, the most popular literary series character to appear in this magazine in the nearly thirty years of its publication history. The first three short novels in her saga have been collected in THE LEGEND OF *SEÑORITA* SCORPION (Circle V Westerns, 1996). The fourth short novel about her, "The Curse of Montezuma," is collected in THE RETURN OF *SEÑORITA* SCORPION: A WESTERN TRIO (Circle V Westerns, 1997). The sixth short novel, comprising the title story, was collected in THE LASH OF *SEÑORITA* SCORPION: A WESTERN TRIO (Circle V Westerns, 1998). The fifth short novel, "The Brand of Penasco," is included in THE SHADOW IN RENEGADE BASIN: A WESTERN TRIO (Five Star Westerns, 2000). In 1946 Malcolm Reiss, who edited *Action Stories*, wanted another *Señorita* Scorpion story, but Savage was too busy, occupied with writing his first hardcover novel, TREASURE OF THE BRASADA (Simon and Schuster, 1947), to produce one that year, although he did complete "The Lash of *Señorita* Scorpion" the next year. Savage wrote the seventh and, as it turned out, final short novel about Elgera Douglas in late May, 1949. He titled the story "Scorpion's Return," and it was purchased by Fiction House on June 1, 1949 for $400.00, at the rate of 2¢ a word. It was published in *Action Stories* (Winter, 1949) under the title "The Sting of *Señorita* Scorpion." This story marked

Savage's last appearance in *Action Stories*. Two issues later, with *Action Stories* (Summer, 1950), the magazine ceased publication. In earlier stories in the saga Chisos Owens, Johnny Hagar, U.S. Marshal Powder Welles, and El Cojo had all fallen in love with Elgera, but ultimately she had to reject each of them for one reason or another. Yet Tony Dexter in this last story may be the chosen one.

I

THE Chisos Mountains rose, smoky and mysterious, through the haze brought by the unseasonal rain beating down upon this borderland marking the southern line of Texas. The woman forced her palomino horse through one of the gorges facing the first foothills of these mountains, her figure bent beneath the driving rain, undistinguishable in great sombrero and yellow slicker.

The gorge rose here, cutting through a high ridge to form a gap. She halted the animal at its high point, turning to look back, something desperate and driven in her face.

Finally she drove the horse on till she found a brush-choked spur cañon and turned the palomino up this till the chaparral hid them from the trail. Here she dismounted and hitched the horse, turning to fight her way back down through rain-bogged clay to a great rock overhanging the main trail. She crawled up this and stretched out on her belly, pulling an Army Colt from its holster.

She did not know how long she had waited there, with the rain pattering mutedly against her slicker, when the man appeared. His horse was as easy to distinguish as her palomino. It was an Appaloosa from the north, its chest a satiny red, fading back to a pure white rump daubed with elongated red spots like spilled paint.

The man's figure was enveloped in a slicker, too, with not much to be seen except its size, immensely broad through the shoulders. His face flickered like dull bronze beneath the brim of his Stetson, turning from one side to the other in constant search. The woman waited till he was directly beneath the rock, then rose to her hands and knees, and jumped with a wild, husky sound.

The man's slicker shrieked with his violent, wheeling motion in the saddle. He had one arm partly thrown up to block when she struck, carrying him off the startled, rearing horse. They hit the ground with a jarring thud. The man was underneath, taking most of the shock. The woman rose to straddle him, laying the barrel of her gun in a hard, calculated blow against the side of his head. His upsurging body stiffened, then sagged back into the rain-beaten mud.

She pulled the Bisley six-gun from its holster beneath his slicker, and stood up. His slicker had come open across his chest, and she saw the star on his vest before he groaned heavily and rolled over on his belly and elbows, shaking his head.

"You stay right there," she told him in a voice trembling with anger. "I'm taking your horse. The nearest human being is about two days' walk from here. I guess you passed there on the way in."

"And by that time, you figure you'll be far enough ahead of me so I'll never catch you," he said.

"I sure do, Marshal," she said.

He rolled over and sat up, looking at her from eyes hooded by anger. "*Señorita* Scorpion," he said, lips twisting sarcastically.

"I prefer my own name," she told him. "Elgera Douglas."

He spat mud, getting to his feet. "I think the Mexicans had a better idea when they called you the Scorpion. And now I've been stung by you. Why the rough stuff? You could have just held the gun on me and asked me to get off my horse."

"I didn't think that would convince you," she said. "I've tried everything in the book and out of it to throw you off my trail these last weeks. I've shot up all the shots in my Winchester, haven't had anything to eat in two days, haven't slept for more than that. You ought to know how desperate a person gets when you drive them up against the wall. I won't stop at hitting you over the head next time, Marshal. . . ."

She halted herself as he took off his mashed Stetson, shaking the mud bitterly from its brim and crown. For the first time, it gave her a clear view of his face. It was a strong, roughly hewn face, black eyes recessed deeply behind heavy, over-hanging brows. The nose had a high, beaked bridge, almost Indian in its shape. Although he had been following her through this country the last two weeks where few men would have bothered shaving, his strong, angular jaw was smooth as copper. He became aware of her surprised attention and lifted his eyes.

"What is it?" he asked.

"You look like . . . like. . . ."

"Billie Dexter?" he said. "I should. He was my brother."

"You're Tony Dexter?"

"Marshal Tony Dexter," he corrected. "Come to take you in for the murder of my brother."

There was an intensely restrained emotion drawing its thread of tremor through his voice when he said this, and the Scorpion could not help the tightening of her face. She understood that smooth jaw now. It was known that Billie Dexter had Indian blood in him; his face had borne the same hawk-like shape, the same lack of hair on the jaw.

The Scorpion settled back a little, her own haunting, obliquely formed face darkening a little. She was a tall girl, made taller by the spike heels of her boots, her legs long and slim in the skin-tight *charro* pants. Her hair, beneath the brim of her sombrero, was as golden as her palomino's mane, her eyes as blue as the Mary color the Mexicans put on their doors.

"I've known it was a government marshal on my trail," she said. "I had no idea it was the brother of Billie Dexter."

His black eyes held a deep, smoldering light. "Won't do you any good to send me back afoot, Scorpion. I'll come back after you again. There isn't anywhere you can go that I won't follow. There isn't a trail you can blot out I won't uncover. I've got enough Comanche in me to follow tracks a lot of men could never find. And I'll follow them till I get you."

"Without ever hearing my side of the story?" she said.

There was no relenting in his face, as he put his hat back on. "You got a side?"

"Billie Dexter was a government surveyor and engineer, come down here to try and find water for the new settlement in Willow Valley," she said. "He also came out to the Santiago to try and help me get water before the dry-up wiped me out. That's why I was with him in George Hall's Land Office at Slickrock. After I left the office, George Hall came back from supper to find Billie dead with a knife in his back, and his papers missing. Is that the way they've got it?"

"You should know," he said.

"Why should I kill him in the middle of town and leave him for everybody to see, when he was out at my ranch for two weeks, thirty miles from civilization?"

She saw the first puzzlement stir in his eyes, to be blotted out deliberately. "I imagine all that will come out at the trial," he said.

"Will it come out why I killed him in the first place?" she asked. Again she saw that change in his eyes, more definable now. "You know just bringing me in won't solve this murder," she said. "You've been trailing me through the Big Bend long enough to know what's going on down here. It started just about the time Billie Dexter came. His reports to the government Land Office in Alpine led them to the official announcement that there would soon be enough water in Willow Valley to supply all the area. Then these hold-ups on the stage started, and the raids on Slickrock. Top that off with enough rustling to force half a dozen of the biggest cattle operators in the district to the wall, and you have something that will ruin the valley before they even get any water. Do you think I'm responsible for all that?"

He shook his head savagely. "Listen. I don't care about that. I saw Billie, lying there in George Hall's Land Office, with that pig-sticker up to its hilt in his back. I think of it every time I think of you. And now that I see you. . . ."

He broke off, breathing heavily, and her own face grew stiff as she spoke again, forcing an even tone into her voice. "Do you think this rustling, this raiding would stop even if you did bring me in? Have you ridden with Sheriff Dennison on any of these posses?"

A faintly puzzled light filled Tony's eyes, before he could

block it off completely. "I was with him a couple of times when he followed the raiders. We got as far as Papago Gap. The trail petered out."

"I thought you could follow any trail," she taunted.

"Maybe I could have followed it," he told her. "Dennison wouldn't even let me try. He said no white man had ever been beyond Papago Gap, to his knowledge. It would be suicide for anyone of known connections with the law to follow the raiders, if they were holed up back there. Two of Dennison's deputies had already disappeared in there."

"Do you think all that is connected with your brother's death?" she asked.

"I'm not interested if it is," he said savagely. "All I'm interested in is bringing my brother's murderess to justice."

"Does Dennison think it's connected with Billie's death?" she insisted.

He tried to meet her eyes with that anger, but his hooded lids fluttered, and dropped. "I suppose he does," Tony said at last, in a guttural way.

"I could go beyond Papago Gap," she told him softly. "My face is on Wanted posters all over the Big Bend."

That anger filled his face again. "You're thinking I'd never get you if you went back in there."

"What's the difference," she said. "The way things stand now, I could go on back in if I felt like it, anyway." She saw that flicker in his eyes again, as he realized she was right, and how it was a break once more in the anger he tried to maintain. She moved in closer to him, ripe underlip forming a pouting curve, blue eyes widening, pleading. "Do you really think I could murder a man . . . that way . . . Marshal?"

His chest lifted with a husky breath. A strange, almost painful, frustration twisted his face. He gave a sudden savage little shake to his head and turned around, walking away from her, to stand facing the wall of the cañon, as if trying to think clearly.

"I should hate you," he said gutturally. "But some of the things you say are too right. This raiding, this rustling is connected with Billie's death somehow. Dennison has suggested the same thing you did . . . that there must be more behind Billie's death than looks on the surface."

She came up behind him, voice husky. "All I'm asking is a chance to prove my innocence, Marshal. Give me your word you'll let me have that chance, and I'll let you have your horse back."

He wheeled around again. Her eyes were half-lidded, like a sleepy child's holding as much promise as plea. The rain pelted softly against the upturned curve of her cheek. Her lips were faintly parted, ripe and red. She saw the dull flush tint his face, and the little pulse begin to beat raggedly against the bronze flesh of his throat.

"Damn you," he said. "All right. I'll give you two weeks. If I haven't heard from you then, one way or the other, I'm coming back after you, Scorpion, and this time I'll get you."

II

THREE days of riding were behind the Scorpion when she came in sight of Papago Gap. She halted her palomino in the evening to stare at the gorge, cutting through the backbone of the Chisos Mountains as if someone had sliced it there with a giant axe. La Rubia's golden hide was whitened with alkali, and the scabbard of the Winchester beneath the woman's left stirrup leather was darkened with sweat. The Scorpion leaned forward in her saddle, free-bitting her horse, with the weariness of the long search behind her.

She rode until the gorge widened into a spot where several spur cañons converged, leaving a broad, sandy cup of a valley. Huddled against the base of the uplift forming the west wall, the Scorpion saw the roof of a mud *jacal* above the level of brush and the posts of a cottonwood corral. She had spent two of the last three nights in the lonely *jacales* of the families who lived their indescribably lonely lives out in these mountains and, with a tired sigh, turned her horse toward this one, thinking of calling on a family's hospitality for a third time.

As she threaded her way from the brush into sight of the crumbling adobe building, a man appeared out of the doorway. He was no different than the others she had seen, small and gaunt, sad of face, dressed in filthy cotton shirt and pants. She saw the suspicion swept from his face by a startled awe as soon as she was close enough for him to recognize her, and, as she swung La Rubia to a halt before him, he said in a shocked way: "*Diablo, señorita.* You cannot be . . . the Scorpion?"

She smiled tiredly at him. "Your people call me that."

The awe was replaced by that suspicion again. "Is it true, *señorita*, that your *rancho* in the Santiago Mountains has been ruined by the drought . . ."—he hesitated—"and that you are wanted for the murder of Billie Dexter, the government surveyor in Slickrock?"

She shrugged. "Would you care?"

A slow grin broke over his face. "They have accused you of many things in the past, *señorita*, unjustly. I do not think such a beautiful woman capable of anything like that. . . ."

"Torbirio," snapped the work-worn woman who had appeared in the doorway, "will you stop making eyes at the *señorita* and ask her to be on her way?"

The man turned toward the woman. "But, Juana, can't you see how tired she is? She must have been riding all day. Cannot we offer her a meal and a bed for the night?"

The woman watched the Scorpion from suspicious eyes, then made a muffled, incoherent sound, turning back into the house. The man turned back, shrugging apologetically.

"*Gracias*," murmured the Scorpion, sliding off the palomino. She stripped off the saddle herself, dropping it just outside the door, against the wall. He led the animal around to the ocotillo corral. She waited till he returned and allowed him to bow her inside. It was only a two-room hovel, the living room typical of these *jacales*—a hard earthen floor beaten to the texture of cement by years of use. There was an *estufa* in one corner, a cone-shaped oven of adobe with banks on either side in which recesses were sunk for pot fires, suspended by a rawhide line from the ceiling. A pot of stew simmered, lifting the appetizing scent of chili to mingle with the acrid reek of boiling chicory coffee.

Three pairs of luminous eyes watched the Scorpion from the doorway leading into the second room. She seated herself cross-legged on one of the faded Indian blankets next to the wall, and the trio of ragged, half-naked children appeared, approaching her cautiously. She smiled warmly, and they gained courage, coming to her, touching her hair in awe, fingering her red blouse curiously, until the Mexican woman ordered them away.

The man got half a dozen horn spoons from a shelf, seating himself opposite the Scorpion. The woman dippered the stew onto wooden platters, bringing it to them, grumbling and muttering under her breath. Accepting one of the spoons, the Scorpion began to eat.

"You'll have to excuse if it is a little sandy," said the man. "Riders coming through the gorge last night knocked off all the chiles we had strung on the corral fence. . . ."

"Torbirio," snapped the woman, wheeling on him angrily.

The man looked at her in surprise. Then a strange expression crossed his face, and, when he turned back, the Scorpion could see how his manner had changed. He seemed uncomfortable in her presence, almost suspicious.

"They couldn't be the gang that held up the Slickrock stage yesterday?" she asked.

"I don't know," answered the man sullenly. "We do not talk about those things here, *señorita*."

"I saw their trail in the gorge," she told him. "It didn't seem to be as many as I suspected. I thought it would be a bigger gang."

"*No sabe*," muttered the man, reverting to his own language. She felt the hostility fill the room, affecting even the children, who began to pull away from her toward their father. It had happened this way with the other families, whenever she had brought up the trouble Willow Valley was experiencing. But now she could not stop. She had come too far, spent too much time already. And if this man knew anything. . . .

"Perhaps some of them were wounded," she offered.

"Not wounded . . . ," the man began, and then checked himself.

"But some were left behind," she said, staring demandingly at him. "That's it, isn't it? What are you hiding? Did one of them lose a horse or something? Are you expecting him through here?"

"*Nada, nada*," said the man angrily, getting to his feet. "Juana, show the *señorita* to her bed. She must be very tired. . . ."

Before he could finish, there was a crashing in the brush outside. The woman darted to the door, with her husband following. The Scorpion jumped to her feet, seeing it over their shoulders. The gorge outside was lighted by a rising moon, revealing the man who came through the mesquite in a stumbling run. He was lean as an alley cat through legs and hips, his torso swelling into chest and shoulders of incredible size, swinging from side to side in a tigerish way with every lunging step he took. His head had a leonine look, shaggy blond hair falling over his eyes. He tried to keep running, but stumbled and went to his hands and knees a few feet from the *jacal*.

"Horse," he gasped. "Got to have a horse. Played out my string. Dennison shot my animal out from under me down by Slickrock. Got another, but I ran it to death a few miles back keeping ahead of the posse. Come on, damn you. Horse, horse. . . ."

The man and woman stood petrified, fear stamped into their faces. The man got to his feet finally, swaying there, and tried to take a step forward. But he fell against the wall, sagging. His ribs swelled and contracted with the air he sucked into his lungs. Seeing how completely drained he was by his exhaustion, the Scorpion snapped: "How many are there in the posse?"

The man turned his gaunt, bony face toward her in surprise. "Three or four was all that lasted this far," he gasped weakly. "They're right behind me."

She could hear the distant pop of brush now and stooped to unlash the sixty-foot rawhide lariat from her saddle, where she had dropped it by the door. She knew they would have no time to get the man on a horse in his state. He was probably too exhausted to ride farther at this point, anyway. She ran through the brush, down the slight incline to the bottom of the gully, where moonlight turned the path of sand to a molten stream. She reached a narrow place in the trail, no more than twenty feet between walls of brush, and lashed one end of the rope about a thick trunk of mesquite.

Then she ran across the trail, playing the rope out at knee height. The earth was shaken now by the pounding of hoofs. She plunged into the brush on the opposite side of the trail, but the horses burgeoned out of the night suddenly, coming at a headlong run, giving her no time to tie the rope on this side. She dropped to a knee, snubbing the rope across her hip.

The first horse hit the rope. The jerk of it almost cut her in two, and she grunted with the effort of keeping upright. With its front hoofs taken from under it, the horse pitched headlong, rider going off with a wild shout. The second horse struck an instant later, and its rider went off over its head. The third and fourth men tried to pull up, but they were too close behind. The third one tripped over the rope, jerking the Scorpion so violently that she was pulled off balance and flung into the sand. The fourth man crashed into the churning rump of the horse ahead, and it threw him off.

The Scorpion came to her feet, pulling at her gun and firing a couple of times to spook the horses farther. The animals were scrambling up now and, one by one, plunged off into the mesquite. Sheriff Dennison was the first man to gain his feet, a kettle-bellied man with flapping, batwing chaps and an alkali-whitened vest of blue serge, his heavy face almost black with rage in this dim light.

"Drop your harness before you get up," she told him.

For a moment, he seemed almost mad enough to go for his gun, anyway. Then his whole body trembling with rage, he unbuckled his holster.

"I see you, Scorpion," he said. "We'll get you. . . ."

"Never mind," she cut him off. "Start your bunch walking. There's a Mexican named Pedro about fifteen miles back. You should make it by morning. He's got horses."

Swearing gutturally, the sheriff turned and led his dazed, sandy men off down the gorge, halting every now and then to stare back. The Scorpion remained there with her gun out till they had disappeared. Then she picked up the four gun belts and, walking heavily under this load of hardware, headed back up the rise toward the *jacal*. She saw now that it was visible from this spot on the trail and knew the people there must have seen what happened. She found one of the spooked horses back in the mesquite and drove him to the *jacal* before her. The big, blond man was still sagged against the wall, grinning at her in amazement.

"*Señorita* Scorpion," he said. "I should have known. I've seen your face on reward dodgers in every town in the Big Bend. But why did you do this?"

"Maybe I need a place to hole up in," she said.

"What makes you think I'd be any good for that?"

"You're with the bunch that's been raiding Slickrock, aren't you?"

"The name is Jesse Cunnard." He grinned.

"Dennison hasn't been able to find where you hole up yet," she told him, unperturbed. "I figured we could make a trade."

"You *did* save my life," he agreed. "I guess I owe you something." He turned his head to look at Papago Gap, a yellow slice in the black chain of the Chisos. "That's why I'll tell you this. Why don't you just let me have the horse and you go on back?"

"I haven't got anywhere to go," she said. "They've pushed me this far already."

"That's Papago Gap," he said, nodding at the notch.

"I know."

"Once beyond that Gap you won't be able to turn back," he said.

"I'll take that chance."

He studied her for a long space of time. "Get your horse, then," he said. "But whatever happens from here on in . . . don't blame me."

III

THEY spent the rest of that night in the *jacal*, for Cunnard was too played out to go on, and then left the next morning. Beyond Papago Gap, the Chisos became mountains out of another world. The haze that made them appear so mysterious from the outside seemed to lower as they were penetrated, until the brush-choked gorges were turned smoky by it, a clinging, mauve smoke, as if the mesquite was on fire, from which the devil's head and the twisted post oaks jumped like empurpled monsters, clawing at legs and hips of the riders. All that day, Jesse Cunnard and the Scorpion threaded the narrow chasms and fought across the knife-edged ridges, coming upon only one water hole in that whole time.

Late afternoon sunlight was slanting down through the jagged peaks of the Chisos when they finally reached the house. It had once been an imposing building in the style of early colonial Spain, with a balcony running across the front over the porch and slotted windows for protection against Apache arrows. There were crumbling walls three feet thick and *viga* poles sticking out at a ceiling level, throwing picket shadow patterns over the sides. Behind were corrals, and the whole was surrounded by high adobe walls with gates of peeled cottonwood that stood open now, sagging forward on their hinges.

A woman came out the front door as Elgera booted her flagging mount through the gate and across the dismal courtyard, where pigs ran loose and chickens scratched for worms. She was a tall, lush-looking woman in a form-fitting green silk dress with a huge jeweled Spanish comb thrust carelessly through a straggling mop of glossy black hair. She stared silently at them out of big, smoldering black eyes.

"Hello, Cora," Cunnard muttered, when they stopped in front of her. "This is Elgera Douglas. She pulled me out of a hole last night."

"Don't you mean *Señorita* Scorpion?" Cora asked sarcastically, letting her eyes travel coldly over Elgera's figure.

"Take it easy," Cunnard said thickly. "I'd never have made it alone. Call Questa and have him take the horses."

Reluctantly Cora turned to look about the littered yard until she saw a lean old Indian squatting down in the shade of a coma tree. The Scorpion expected her to call, but she only picked up a stone and threw it in the Indian's direction. It skittered over the ground, flinging dirt into his face, and he looked up in surprise. Cora gestured for him to come over and pointed to the sweat-channeled palomino. "He can't hear and he can't talk," Cora said disgustedly. "He can't do anything else, either."

The old Indian stood up and stared toward them. The Scorpion saw that he was tall and that he wore his tattered rawhide garments with the remnants of a fine dignity. His head, with its thick mane of white hair, caught back in a blue-beaded head band was carried high, and, although his step was slow, it was still proud. She slipped from La Rubia, handing him the reins with a smile.

For an instant, she seemed to see surprise in his eyes. It puzzled her a moment. Before she could define it, Cunnard dismounted and dropped his reins, and Cora turned to lead them into the house. The front room ran the length of the house, a huge adobe fireplace at one end and a two-foot *banca* running around the walls to form a combination shelf and bench, covered with blankets and pottery and riding gear. The furniture was heavy and ancient, high-backed and ornate in the tradition of colonial Spain. Innumerable niches recessed the walls, in which stood the wooden *santos* carved by the loving hands of long-dead *peones*, and some of the *savanarillas* serving as tapestries bore the mark of exquisite weaving. It all formed an air of elegant decadence, as of a once regal house gone to ruin.

The Scorpion became aware of the man sitting in one of the immense chairs by the fireplace, an enormously fat man in a monogrammed silk shirt and imported whipcords, every fat finger loaded with rings of diamond and jade and turquoise that flashed and gleamed in the light from the flickering fire. He bent forward in the chair without offering to rise, glittering little eyes licking up the turn of the Scorpion's lithe legs in their tight *charro* pants and the curve of her breast under her ducking jacket. A sly, pawky smile formed its crease in his puffy cheeks.

"The Thcorpion," he lisped. "How fabulouth. You honor the houth of Elijah Maine."

Cunnard's face darkened at the mockery in Maine's voice. "Cut it out, Elijah," he said. "She pulled me out of a hole. I was at the end of my rope, and Dennison would have nabbed me if it hadn't been for her."

Maine settled back in his chair, studying Cunnard with narrowing eyes. At this moment, another man came from a door leading into a hall and stopped short, mouth dropping in surprise. He was a square-set, vicious-looking Mexican, shoulders bulging like sides of beef beneath his polka-dot shirt.

"*Santo*," he said softly. "It is like seeing a ghost. We thought you was done for good, Jesse."

Cunnard turned to him, anger fighting his reckless, gray eyes. "You mean *hoped* I was done, don't you, Charlie?"

"Now don't talk like that, Jesse. . . ."

"You didn't have to pull out," said Cunnard, in growing heat. "Dennison wasn't even in sight."

"But we couldn't find you in the brush, Jesse. . . ."

"With me shooting my head off?" snarled Cunnard. "You've been wanting to rod this bunch for a long time, Charlie. Ten to one it was at your suggestion they pulled out."

Charlie pulled a needle-pointed *belduque* from his belt, and began to throw it up in the air, allowing the hilt to slap into his palm. "So it was my suggestion," murmured Charlie in a soft, baiting voice. "I think you would have pulled out and left me, under the same circumstances."

"I will next time, you can bet your bottom dollar. . . ."

"Gentlemen, gentlemen," placated Maine. "We might ath well dithband now, if we're going to be at each otherth' throath all the time. We'll never get anything done that way. I don't think you've met the Thcorpion yet, Charlie. It ith theldom that we have thuch illuthtriuth guethth in our humble ethtablithment."

Charlie let his glittering eyes swing around until they rested on the Scorpion, and a leering smile spread his lips. "Ah-h-h," he said in whispered appreciation. "I should have known. I have heard so many stories about you I did not really believe you existed, *señorita*. The *peones* around Terlingua swear they have seen you change from a woman into a scorpion before their very eyes. Is that true?"

Elijah Maine chuckled softly. "Forgive our Charlie, Thcorpion. He muth have hith little joketh."

"Cut it out," Cunnard told them roughly.

"What's the matter, Jesse?" Cora asked in a thin sarcasm.

Charlie moved toward the Scorpion, still flipping the knife absently. "I have heard men will die *for* your sting, as well as *of* it, *señorita*," he said. He had come within one pace of her, and he took that in a swift, surprising lunge, slipping his free arm about her waist before she could stop him and wheeling her back into the wall, his voice guttural and demanding. "Sting me," he said. "Sting me, *señorita*."

Her hand flashed up to claw his face, but he blocked it. Before he could put his lips to hers, he was wrenched from her violently and whirled around. She saw that Cunnard had grabbed one arm, and was spinning him. Charlie tried to regain balance, slashing wildly with his knife.

Cunnard blocked that arm, tearing the knife from his grasp as if he had been a baby, and then used Charlie's original momentum to hurl him on around and let him go.

Charlie went helplessly across the width of the room, smashed into the wall, and then crumpled down onto the floor. Face purple with rage, Cunnard took the knife blade in his two hands and snapped it. He dropped it to the floor. The Scorpion saw that it had cut his hands, but he did not even seem to notice the blood. His rage swelled his throat till his voice was hardly intelligible.

"Next time you put your hands on her, I'll snap you like that," he told the dazed Charlie. "I told you she saved my life. You're going to treat her right."

"Maybe it's more than the fact that she saved your life, Jesse," Cora murmured in that soft, vindictive sarcasm.

"Maybe it is," he snarled, whirling on her. "What's it to you?"

Cora stiffened under his savage voice. The blood drained from her face till it had a whipped look. "You'll be sorry for that, Jesse," she said in a rended, whispering voice.

"I'm tired of you children thpatting like thith," lisped Elijah peevishly. "Go tell Quethta to get dinner ready, Cora." Cora did not seem to hear him. She was still staring at Cunnard in that white-faced rage. Elijah seemed to swell a little in the chair, and his voice lowered till it was hardly audible, the lisp more marked than ever. "I thaid tell Quethta to get dinner ready, Cora."

Cora's whole body twitched slightly. She turned her glance toward her father, and the Scorpion saw that rage washed out by something else, almost a fear. Then Cora turned stiffly and went to a hall door, disappearing.

"Pleath thit down," Elijah told the Scorpion. "Charlie, tell the retht of the men dinner will be ready thoon."

Cunnard paced restlessly to a cut-glass decanter on the side table and poured himself a stiff drink, then sought a chair near the fire, dropping down into it and stretching his long legs out in animal relaxation. The fire glinted in his shaggy, blond hair and played fitfully over his irregular features, catching violent little lights in his eyes. The Scorpion could not deny that he was handsome, in a wild, animal way.

Elijah began chuckling slyly. "I have heard tho much about you, my dear. Thith latht venture particularly interethted me. Why on earth thould you want to kill thuch a nithe, harmleth young man ath Billie Dexter?"

The Scorpion studied his face, hunting for guile, wondering if any of them knew who really had killed Billie Dexter. "You knew Billie?" she asked.

The man spread his fat hands ruefully. "He wath our guetht while he wath up here, looking for the water." He began chortling again in that sibilant, smug way. "And now it ith you who knowth where the water ith."

"What brings you to that conclusion?" asked the Scorpion.

The man had no eyebrows. They were merely sallow ridges of flesh, bald and fat as a baby's bottom, lifting in mild surprise. "But why elthe thould you kill Billie Dexter? Rumor had it that it wath not actually a map he made that thowed the location of the water. More of a log, naming variouth landmarkth by which you could locate the approximate courthe of the underground river."

"I've heard the rumors," murmured the Scorpion.

"Ah?" Elijah's eyes raised again, and he glanced at Cunnard and began laughing, as if at some secret.

Cora had come back in now and sullenly began to set the table at the other end of the room. Charlie entered from the rear with two other men. Elijah introduced them to the Scorpion as Peel Forman and Zamora. Zamora was a tall, skinny Mexican in brush-scarred *mitaja* leggin's who immediately sprawled out on the floor, against the *banca*, and began to strum idly at a guitar with only three strings remaining. Peel Forman was an indescribably filthy man, his Levi's and ducking jacket blackened with grease and dirt and droppings. He hunkered down to his heels against the wall, watching the Scorpion from blank, unreadable eyes, idly picking the lice from his matted beard. Questa padded in with a great platter of mutton and tortillas, and the men began taking their places at the table. The Scorpion found a chair at one end with Cora on her left. Elijah toyed with one of the heavy silver beakers while Questa served.

"Frankly," murmured Elijah, "I think the rumor of Billy Dexter'th map ith ath unfounded ath the legendth of that underground river. Billie went right back to Thlickrock from here. He thowed no thignth of having dithcovered the river when he left here. That thtory of underground water in the Chithoth ith ath old ath the mountainth themthelveth. Who'th ever found it? They thay the Indianth know. Wouldn't they have uthed it, if they did? I bought thith plathe for a thong from Don Bacardo, an old Mexican, whoth father had owned half the Chithoth on a grant from the Thpanith Crown. Would Don Bacardo have thold that cheaply if there wath water here? Thith land would be pritheleth if it were irrigated. It would be the betht cattle country in the world. . . ."

A sharp cry from Cora cut him off. Questa had come in from behind to serve her, and she had been so intent upon what her father was saying that she had not noticed the Indian. As he bent down, a movement of her head must have tilted the plate of meat, spilling the juice over her.

"You fool!" she cried, pushing him violently away. "You've burned me."

Stumbling under the push, he dropped the platter, spilling all of its contents down onto her. With the scream of an enraged cat, Cora caught one of the heavy silver beakers off the table and swung it at Questa's head. He staggered backwards, tripping and falling to his hands and knees, blood spurting from the cut on his head.

Eyes blank with rage, Cora leaped after him, cup raised to strike again. The Scorpion had already slid her chair back, drawing her gun at the same time. The shot blotted out Cora's wild voice. The bullet hit the silver beaker while Cora's hand was still upraised, smashing it from her fingers. Cora made an explosive, startled sound of pain, hugging the numbed hand into her, and wheeled to stare at the Scorpion in shocked surprise. That was swept away before a new rage that turned her eyes to black pools of hatred in her white, contorted face.

"Damn you . . . !"

"Cora," Elijah snapped. His high, lisping voice halted her like a whip. She was held suspended there, her whole body trembling. Finally she settled back on her heels. The fat man chuckled indulgently. "That ith right, m' dear. I'd hate to thee my own daughter thot, now, wouldn't I?"

Cora's voice escaped her like a hiss of steam, between her clenched teeth. "You aren't going to let her. . . ."

"On the contrary," Maine murmured, "I'm not going to let *you!* Thee undoubtedly thaved Quethta'th life. Another blow from that beaker and you would have killed him. We couldn't have that happen to our faithful old retainer, could we? No, of courthe not. Pleathe go to your room, Cora, and change your dreth, and be prepared to exude nothing but thweetness and light when you return."

Cora stared at her father for a long instant, while the candlelight flickered over the voluptuous cruelty of her face. Finally, lips working soundlessly, she wheeled and left the room. The Scorpion holstered her gun, turned to see Questa rising shakily to his feet. His eyes were on her. She had never seen such dog-like gratitude expressed by a human being before. Then Jesse Cunnard's husky, mordant laugh rustled from the other end of the table.

"You've got a slave for yourself, Scorpion," he said. "Questa knows you saved his life. Nobody else ever done anything like that for him. You're probably the first person he ever met who didn't haul off and kick him just for spite."

She moved restlessly in her chair, disturbed, embarrassed, by that melting, awed adoration in the Indian's eyes. As he shuffled from the room, she became aware of

Elijah Maine, watching her. Suddenly he threw back his head and began to laugh, shrill, feminine squeals of sound that shook his whole body until he choked upon it, and started coughing. He took up a beaker of wine to stop this, spilling it all over his shirt front. Still choking, he set it down and dabbed in peevish anger at the stain.

Questa cleaned up the mess and got more food from the kitchen. It was a weird, strained dinner for the Scorpion. Cora came back finally in a different gown and seated herself sullenly at the table, to finish her meal without speaking.

When the Scorpion was through, she asked Elijah if she might be shown to a room. He made a casual sign to Questa, and the old Indian padded into the hall, leading the Scorpion down the dark passage and up a flight of stairs to another hall, lined with doors. After opening one for her, he turned, catching at her wrist. His lips worked soundlessly, his whole face twisted. She put a hand to his arm, trying to think of some way of communication. It was obvious he wanted to tell her something. At last, with a frustrated, fearful look darkening his eyes, he turned to scurry off down the hall.

The Scorpion entered the room, propping a chair under the doorknob. There was no way to latch the shutters on the windows, however. She feared falling asleep, but she knew she could not remain awake much longer, with the exhaustion of the last days weighing her down. She put her gun under the pillow, and lay down with her hand on the butt. Wind whispered through the ocotillo corral outside. The house was filled with mysterious murmurings. She had the feeling that sleep would be dangerous, yet she knew she could not remain awake all night. The days of constant riding behind her seemed to have piled up suddenly into overpowering weariness. She sank into it without a struggle.

She seemed to dream, and then the dreams seemed to take focus, and become sounds, and she woke to this. No telling how long she had been asleep. The room was black. The wind had died outside. Then she knew what had awakened her.

The soft, scraping sound came again. It was right above her bed. There was an exhalation, clothing rustling with the violence of movement. Clutching for the Colt beneath her pillow, the Scorpion rolled herself off the edge of the bed, knowing the blow would be coming from above. She went into a body, jackknifing it over her. At the same time, there was a sharp ripping of cloth at her back, and she knew a knife had sunk into the mattress where her own body had been a moment before.

She hooked one leg off onto the floor as she fell, driving on against that body. But it whirled away, leaving her plunging against space. She struck the floor rolling and came up against the chest against the wall. There was a clatter of shutters. She went over on an elbow, raising her gun, but whoever it was had already gotten through the window, leaving an empty, yellow rectangle of moonlight.

The Scorpion got to her feet and ran over there, climbing through the window and onto the balcony. This was empty, although the windows of other rooms opened out onto it. Through the spindled railings, she could see the empty courtyard below, and hear the restless stirring of horses in the corrals. The Chisos Mountains towered vindictively into a depthless sky. She leaned against the wall, gun in hand, staring up at their brooding countenance and realizing, for the first time, how alone she was.

IV

THE Scorpion did not sleep much the rest of that night. Dawn found her pacing the room, hollow-eyed and tense with strain. The sun rose brazenly over the jagged peaks of the Chisos behind the house, flooding her chamber with bright light. She heard stirrings in the rooms on either side of her, and a voice downstairs. Then, at the window, she caught sight of Questa in the courtyard.

He was standing in a strange, rigid position, feet planted solidly against the earth, head lifted. His eyes were closed, and there was a strange rapt expression on his face. It reminded her of a hound dog when it sensed something beyond the ken of human beings.

She watched him for three or four minutes, and then she caught sight of a rider coming through the sagging gate. It struck her that somehow Questa had known this man was coming. It sent a strange, eerie chill up her back. She bent forward, eyes widening with surprise, as she saw that the rider was George Hall, the government Land Office man from Slickrock. He got off his jaded horse, a tall, somber man in black broadcloth, knees and elbows and cuffs whitened with alkali. The weariness of the long ride drew his cheeks in till there were deep hollows beneath his high, sharp cheek bones. As Questa came forward to take his horse, Hall turned toward the front door. There was a muted creaking of that portal, and then the lisping voice of Elijah Maine.

"Good morning, George. You're early. You mutht have

ridden all night."

"I did," said Hall dryly. "And I'm in no good mood, Elijah. That last job on the Slickrock stage was too sloppy."

"But Jethe and the boyth took care of it jutht ath you thaid. He told me he left the thtage burned and the hortheth run off, and the pathengerth had to walk twenty mileth into Thlickrock. It won't take many more of thothe attackth to make Bruno Hollman loothe hith franchithe on the road. Then Thlickrock will be cut off from any regular connectionth with the outthide."

"And everybody will know that's exactly what we intended," growled Hall. "Cunnard didn't even attempt to make it look like an ordinary hold-up. He left those mailbags strewn around in the road without opening a one. Didn't even shoot open the strongbox."

"But we knew they weren't carrying any cath thith time. . . ."

"That's not the point," Hall told him.

Elijah's chuckle floated up to the Scorpion, soft and oily. "Of courthe it ithn't, George," he said. "Tho the boyth were a little hathty. Maybe they were getting a little anxiouth about their money. You haven't been up in two weekth, you know."

Their voices faded inside.

Quickly the Scorpion took the chair from under her doorknob and moved down the hall to the head of the stairs, where a balcony overlooked the lower room. She could see Hall, seating himself sourly in a chair before the cold fireplace, thrusting long, lean legs out before him to stretch the saddle stiffness from them.

"We'll have breakfatht in a while," Elijah told him,

seating himself opposite the man. "How are the other thingth coming?"

"Peterson is just about ready to sell out his Double Sickle," Hall muttered. "This rustling has bled him white. His price is five thousand. That's not a tenth of what it'll be worth when we get that water. I still don't want my name involved. We'll have the deed signed over to you as usual. I've deposited five thousand dollars in your account in the Alpine bank. You write out a check for that, and I'll take it to Peterson."

"What about the other money?" fretted Elijah.

"Your men will get paid," Hall told him irritably, patting his breast pocket. "And I've got another job for them. Norden Halleck has shipped in some well-digging equipment. He's storing it in the old Warren barn in Slickrock. The barn's too heavily guarded for me to do anything. They've got Dennison and his whole crew around the place, as well as Tony Dexter. . . ."

"The marthal?" asked Elijah sharply.

Hall's brows raised in some surprise. "Yeah. What are you all so spooked of him for?"

Elijah shook his head, frowning darkly. "You ought to know by now. He ithn't any ordinary marthal. He'th wild, Hall. He'th dangerouth. Better not even tell the boyth he'th there. I don't know if I could even get them to go."

Hall shrugged. "All right. What I want you to do is burn that barn and the equipment in it."

"What good would well-digging equipment do Halleck?" asked Elijah. "I thought you were the only one who knowth where the water ith?"

Hall rose, paced restlessly across the room. "Perhaps I

am. But I don't want to take a chance on Halleck or any-body else finding it till we're ready."

"Perhapth you don't know where the water ith," offered Elijah.

Hall wheeled on him, a strange, taut expression on his face. "Now what makes you say that?"

Whatever Elijah answered was blotted out from the Scorpion's ears by Cora's voice, coming softly, vindic-tively from behind her. "Eavesdropping?"

The Scorpion wheeled to see her standing there in a wrapper, eyes heavy-lidded from recent sleep, ripe lips twisted in hatred. "Go downstairs," she told the Scorpion. "Father will be glad to know you're interested."

The Scorpion knew how useless refusal would be. She shrugged and went on downstairs with Cora following. She saw the surprise in Hall's face as she appeared. Elijah turned in his chair, smiling.

"Ah, yeth. Here ith thomeone elthe who ith thupposed to know where the water ith."

"The Scorpion?" asked Hall sharply.

"Why look tho thurprithed, George?" asked Elijah. "Thee killed Billie Dexter, didn't thee? Why elthe thould thee do that unleth to get the map of the underground river?"

A new interest kindled in Hall's eyes. "You've got it?" he asked the Scorpion.

Her blue eyes grew opaque, and she shrugged. "Maybe I just didn't like the way Billie parted his hair."

Hall whirled to Elijah. "If she's got it, why don't you make her give it to you?"

"Why thould we, George?" asked Elijah with an insid-ious grin. "Ath long ath you know where it ith, anyway?"

Hall settled back, a furtive light moving through his eyes. He shrugged against his chair, frowned at the Scorpion. "How did she find this place? How did she get here?"

"Thee saved Jethe'th life the other day," Elijah told him.

"You aren't going to let her stay?" asked Hall.

Elijah pursed his lips. "Why not? Thee'th wanted by the law. Thee pulled Jethe out of a hole. Why not let her ride with him? Thee's amazing with a gun, George. Thee'd be worth any three men on a job like thith one coming up."

"But how can you trust her?" asked Hall.

"Why not let her prove herthelf?" asked Elijah.

"No." Hall shook his head sharply. "I say no."

"I say yes." Jesse Cunnard told them, coming down the stairs. He reached the bottom and spread his feet, tucking thumbs into his belt, and swaggering there. "Did I hear somebody say anything else?"

"Listen, Jesse," Hall told him. "Why take chances? How do we know where she stands?"

"She can't stand anywhere but with us. Her face is on Wanted posters all over the Big Bend. I'm asking you once more, George. I say yes . . ."—Cunnard bent toward him, smoky eyes stirred by violent little lights—"do I hear anybody say no?"

"All right. Hell! All right." Hall waved his hand viciously, not wanting to meet Cunnard's eyes. "Go ahead and put your neck in a noose. I don't give a damn."

Cunnard threw back his head, shaking the room with that wild, wolfish laughter. "That's fine, George, that's just fine. Now, let's have some breakfast. I'm hungrier'n seven coyotes starved all year."

While they ate, Hall told them just what he wanted done

in Slickrock, and paid them off. One by one, Zamora and Charlie and Peel Forman trooped out to saddle up. The Scorpion and Cunnard were last, leaving Hall with Elijah and Cora still at the table. A portal ran the length of the front of the house, supported by *puntales* of peeled cedar, and at the end of this arcade, hidden yet from the corrals, Cunnard stopped the Scorpion.

"Nobody's asked you yet, how you feel about riding with us?"

Her ripe lower lip pouted. "They can only hang me once, and they already want to do that."

He laughed deeply in his chest. It played across her nerves like the fingers of a hand. She could not deny the animal magnetism of him, standing there so close to her, like a big, shaggy, blond beast. His gunsmoke eyes played over her body, and he reached up one forefinger to scratch at his jaw.

"See Questa in the courtyard this morning?" he asked.

"What was he doing?" she said. "He seemed to know that Hall was coming."

"He can feel the vibrations of a horse coming up that knoll while it's still too far away for you to hear it," Cunnard said.

"I've heard the deaf or blind develop their other senses to an incredible degree in compensation," she told him.

He nodded. "These Indians are pretty primitive. All his senses were probably much more developed than ours to begin with. That's what Billie Dexter claimed, anyway."

"Billie Dexter?"

"Sure. Elijah told you Billie stayed here while he was hunting for that water. He was the only one besides you that Questa has ever taken to. I guess that's because nobody else has ever been kind to the Indian. Billie took him out a lot of times to guide him through these mountains."

Her lips parted. "Were you here then?"

"Now, why should that matter?" he grinned. Then the grin became a chuckle. "You're beautiful when you're excited. Your lips glisten like they're wet. You looked that way when you shot the beaker out of Cora's hand last night. Wild. Like a cat or something. I like that. I guess you've never been tamed, have you?"

"That's one way of putting it," she told him.

Before she could block it, he had one arm about her waist and was pinning her back against the wall of the house. She lashed up to hit him, but he blocked it. Then his lips were on hers, sensual, demanding. She was surprised at how she reacted to that magnetism in him, meeting the kiss for a moment, unable to help herself. Then she recovered, and got her free arm between them, hooking a leg back of his knee and shoving. He had to jump backward and release her to keep from being tripped. One of the *puntales* stopped him, and he stood against this cedar support, chest rising and falling heavily, laughing at her, deeply in his throat. Then he sobered abruptly, his glance sliding off to the side.

It made her turn, her eyes finding Cora in the door of the house. The woman's face was dead white. Her eyes glowed like coals, settling on the Scorpion for a moment. Then without a word she wheeled, and disappeared inside.

"We'd better go," Cunnard said in a dark voice. "I'd hate to have Cora look at me that way."

V

THE ride to Slickrock took most of the day. The Scorpion made careful note of the trail they used, filing each landmark away in her memory. They passed through Papago Gap about two that afternoon. Shadows were long when they finally emerged from the last narrow cañon out into benchlands that overlooked Willow Valley.

The town lay in the northern tip of the valley, its single main street forming a dusty track through parallel lines of buildings. It had originally been a Mexican village of squalid adobe hovels scattered around the usual plaza. Now, with the influx of settlers and ranchers, new frame structures had risen. The Warren barn was the oldest frame in town, its hip roof towering above the adobes flanking it on either side. It lay toward the north end of Slickrock, near the original plaza, and faced the Topaz Saloon across the street. As the dusty file of riders pulled up to view this, Hall told them: "I'll leave you now. Make this better than that stagecoach job."

Cunnard stared at him without answering. Casting a narrow-lidded glance at the Scorpion, Hall reined his animal off down a cut-off trail that approached town from a different direction than they would take.

"You really think he knows where that underground river is, Jesse?" Zamora asked.

"He wouldn't be doing all this if he didn't, would he?" Cunnard told him. "Anyway, Billie Dexter worked out of the Land Office. If he found it, George Hall had the best chance of anyone of knowing." His saddle creaked, as he shifted to scan the street. "Here's what we'll do. The bunch of you head straight down the main street from the south, shooting and yelling and making as big a ruckus as you can. That will draw the men guarding the barn around to the front. Meanwhile, I'll come in from the north, and catch that alley going down behind the barn. There's hay lofts at the rear, and it ought to fire up quick. Once that barn starts, I don't think they have enough water in town to stop it. As soon as you see smoke, fade out into those alleys opposite from the barn. If I haven't met you there five minutes after the barn is burning, light a shuck for these benches." He turned to Charlie, grinning wickedly. "And if I'm not here, don't worry. I'm not giving anybody a chance to run out on me, today."

Charlie met his eyes a moment, then wheeled his buckskin viciously on down the trail. The others followed, with the Scorpion bringing up the rear. There was enough mesquite and chaparral on the flats to shield their approach, as long as they stayed off the main road. The clank of a blacksmith's hammer reached them through the sultry, deepening twilight of early evening. A creaking wagon passed them, just out of sight on the road.

They pulled out onto that road within a hundred yards of the first buildings flanking the town's main street. Charlie pulled his gun, and raised it to fire. It set the bunch of them off, yelling and whooping and shooting as they broke down the street into town. An ancient Mexican leaped from his rocker before an adobe store, upsetting the chair as he scrambled for the door. The blacksmith came running from his forge, a cherry-red horseshoe still held in tongs. He dropped the shoe and ducked back inside as Zamora took a shot at him.

A man had been walking down the line of buildings toward the sheriff's office, carrying a Henry repeater. He started running for a doorway, then must have decided he could not make it. He wheeled around to face the street, back flat against the wall, and began firing and levering his Henry as fast as he could. On his third or fourth shot, Charlie's horse stumbled and veered sharply aside, running blindly at a building with a wooden overhang.

Zamora wheeled in the saddle, emptying his six-gun into the man with the Henry. The man slid down the wall, with the bullet holes appearing one by one in the adobe behind him.

Charlie had not been able to turn his frenzied, wounded horse aside. As it plunged in under the overhang, he kicked free of his stirrups and made a cat-like leap up from the saddle. The edge of the overhang caught his belly. The horse went out from under him, running in under the wooden awning to smash headlong into the wall, leaving Charlie hanging there. From windows across the streets, men began to take pot shots at him. Peel Forman pulled his horse onto its haunches and wheeled it to face those windows, systematically raking them with his pair of six-guns held at hip height. The shots from that direction ceased.

Charlie swung one leg up onto the slanting overhang, and started crawling up this for the protection of the roof. He bellied over the foot-high parapet these adobe walls formed above the roof level, and lay down behind this. The Scorpion could see his gun lying out in the middle of the street.

Forman had wheeled to charge his horse on down toward the barn now, with Zamora in his wake. The Scorpion brought up the rear. At this moment, they passed the first intersection and bore down upon the barn in the middle of the next block. Sheriff Dennison and two other men had taken refuge behind water troughs and feed barrels and were opening fire, and more men were running down the passage from the rear of the barn.

One of Dennison's shots spilled Zamora's horse from beneath him. The skinny Mexican kicked free of his plunging animal, setting up a cloud of dust as he hit the rutted street, and rolled. The Scorpion saw his gun fly from his hand. He came up hard against a curb, rising to his hands and knees in a dazed way, and looked out at his gun in the middle of the street. The firing was getting heavier now, however, and he was forced to run for the cover of a building.

"Drag your horse in on this other side!" Peel Forman shouted at the Scorpion, spinning his mount on a heel to gallop into an alley on the opposite side of the street from the barn. The Scorpion had not seen Tony Dexter yet, however, and figured he must still be at the rear of the barn. The building flanking the barn was a long, low structure of adobe, formerly a ranch house converted into an office building for the valley cattlemen's association. There was a narrow passageway between this and the next building that penetrated to the alley behind. The Scorpion wheeled her horse off the street and into this dark passage, running the palomino down its length to the narrow, rutted alley behind. This was the alley that Cunnard meant to come down, but she could not see him yet.

She swung off La Rubia, dropping her reins to the ground, and darted across the rear of the adobe office building. There were greening willows and cottonwoods here, along a spindled fence, and she used them for cover, quickly approaching the passageway between this building and the barn. From behind a tree here, she could see the last of the excited guards running down the passageway toward the street and could hear the rolling bellow of shots out there, and Dennison's hearty, cursing voice.

A sinking sensation chilled her, as she saw this. She had hoped to catch at least one of them before he left the rear. Then she stiffened, with the feel of a gun in her ribs.

"Drop your gun, Elgera," said Tony Dexter in a soft, dangerous voice. "Nobody's starting anything from this end."

She dropped her Colt, then wheeled to stare up at him, panting: "That's what I came back here to tell you. You've got to get the rest of these men back here. The bunch attacked from the front to pull you around so Cunnard could start a fire back here."

"That's what I figured," Tony told her. "I planted myself behind that fence for just that purpose. I'm also figuring something else. Maybe it wasn't Cunnard they told to light a fire back here. Maybe it was you."

"No, Tony," she pleaded. "You've got to get the rest of them back here. Please. Cunnard will be here at any minute. . . ."

She broke off at the ground-shaking thunder of hoofs, and Jesse Cunnard broke into view around a turn in the alley, coming from the north end. Tony swung the Scorpion out of the way so hard she went into the wall, smashing her head against it. The world seemed to spin, and the earth hit her face. Dazed, she rolled over to see that Cunnard had started to pull up his horse. But he did not have his gun out, and that would make him too good a target for the marshal. Instead of stopping, he slackened the reins and spurred the beast back into its headlong run, directly at Tony, bending low so that the front of the animal blocked him off from the marshal.

Tony tried to jump aside and get a clear shot at Cunnard without hitting the horse, but he was pinched in against the trees and wall of the building. The animal swept into him, shoulder spinning him back into the wall, knocking the gun from his hand. With his other hand, he made a desperate grab for Cunnard's leg, as the horse went on by.

Cunnard tried to kick free, drawing at his gun. But Tony hung on, unbalancing him in the saddle, and Cunnard spilled off the rump of the plunging horse. He hit hard, knocking the air out of him. But he hung onto his gun, now out of its holster. Gasping heavily, he rolled over and tried to line it up on Tony.

The marshal himself had been thrown from his feet by the violence of hanging onto Cunnard that way, but he was close enough to lash out with a boot, catching Cunnard's hand with a sharp heel and knocking the six-gun from it. With a snarl, Cunnard came to his hands and knees, reaching for the weapon with his other hand. But Tony rolled over and lunged at him, carrying him back away from the gun. At the same time, Zamora appeared from the passageway between the offices and the bank. He still had the gun in his hand, and there was a wild look to his face. When he saw Cunnard and the marshal rolling across the ground, he ran full tilt at them, and jumped at Tony's back just as he came up.

For a moment, after Zamora hit, there was a confused

tangle of arms and legs, and a sudden, gasping grunt from one of them. Still dazed from that blow on the head, the Scorpion crouched on her hands and knees, trying to find the strength to rise. She knew that if she helped Tony now, it would reveal her to the others, and, if any of them got out of this alive, she could not go back to the Maine house as one of them. Then, from the corner of her eye, she saw a head bobbing on the rooftop off to her left and turned to see Charlie, coming from the roof of that building that he had gained from the overhang. He stopped at its edge, staring across the narrow passageway between it and the adobe, one-story bank. Then, with a grunt audible to the Scorpion, he made the jump.

At the same moment, Tony came up from beneath Zamora and Cunnard, slugging and kicking. Zamora caught him from behind, pinning his arms, as he gained his feet. But Cunnard was only on his knees in front of Tony, grappling with him, and Tony got one leg free, jamming the boot in Cunnard's chest and kicking him over onto his back.

Then the marshal gave a great, grunting heave, tearing one of his arms loose, and jabbed that elbow into Zamora's gut. The Mexican doubled over helplessly. Tony wheeled and threw himself at the man, carrying him back into the wall of the building so hard great cracks appeared in the adobe, spiderwebbing away from Zamora's body. Cunnard was on his feet now, and Tony whirled to meet him.

They looked like two great animals to the Scorpion. Tony's broad shoulders rising and falling heavily as he sucked breath into his great, arched chest, his big frame braced against the wall to meet Cunnard's charge, his black hair falling in long, sweat-slickened shanks over his bronze face. And Cunnard, coming up to his feet and launching himself at Tony with a hoarse, gusty bellow, had smoky eyes flecked with rage.

Cunnard drove for Tony's belly with a shoulder, and Tony twisted aside to block it with a hip. Cunnard's body crashed against him, driving him back into the wall. Tony brought a vicious, chopping blow down to the back of Cunnard's neck, but the man twisted over, throwing up an arm to block it, and with his grappling hold on Tony's hip twisted the marshal away from the wall. They staggered out into the alley, leaving Zamora lying half conscious at the base of the wall, moaning softly.

The Scorpion finally found the will to move, and crawled to where Tony's gun lay, picking it up and rising to her feet. She saw Charlie jumping from the bank to this building now, a knife in his hand.

Tony and Cunnard had regained their balance out in the alley and were toe to toe, slugging it out. Tony blocked one of Cunnard's blows and came inside, sinking his fist into the man's belly. Cunnard gasped sharply, trying to shift in and ride Tony for a moment. Tony would not grapple with him, knocking him away with another blow.

Cunnard bent forward, both arms thrown up in defense. Tony caught one, tearing it aside to open the man up, and caught him on the side of the head with a blow that spun him halfway around. Tony followed that up, hitting him in the belly again. Doubled over, Cunnard staggered into the wall. It was the only thing that kept him from falling.

He recovered himself there, met Tony's rush with his arms covering him. One of Tony's blows glanced off his elbow, and Cunnard lunged forward to strike before Tony could cover up. His fist caught Tony in the ribs, knocking him back in a wheeling, spinning way. Cunnard plunged away from the wall to follow it up.

But Tony got his feet under him and met the man's wild, incautious rush with a calculated one-two that sent Cunnard staggering back against the wall. Tony followed him in, driving heavy, desperate punches to the man's head and body, letting out a great, hoarse gasp of air with the effort of each blow.

The first one stiffened Cunnard against the wall. The second one doubled him over. His knees buckled, and he began to slide, hugging his arms in close, desperately trying to cover himself. The third blow tore those arms wide, leaving his belly unprotected. Tony followed it up with one that caught that belly deep, emptying all the air from Cunnard. Face drained to a ghastly pallor, mouth wide open, eyes glazed, Cunnard hung there. The next blow would put him out for good, and Tony brought his right back for a short, vicious uppercut.

At that same moment there was the soft patter of feet on the roof, and Charlie appeared, crouched, a knife in his hand, ready to jump. The Scorpion's gun arm lifted with the impulse to shoot. But, again, she knew it would ruin her chances of remaining one of them if she revealed her sympathies now. Yet she knew Charlie had every chance of killing Tony, jumping down on him with the knife that way. With a wild little cry, she did the only thing left, jumping in behind Tony before Charlie could leap and hitting the marshal neatly over the head.

His fist stopped halfway to Cunnard's jaw. He hung there for a moment, then his great frame collapsed at the Scorpion's feet. Charlie caught himself leaping, remaining suspended there a moment, looking down in surprise.

"Why did you do that now?" he asked. "I could have slit his throat so easy."

Zamora had come around and was getting sickly to his feet. "Listen, we got to get out of here. Peel ain't going to hold them much longer out front. He faded into an alley on the other side, but I couldn't make it."

Cunnard was straightening slowly against the wall, a sick, drained look to his face. He sucked in air, trying to speak, but nothing would come out. Charlie turned around and slid over the edge of the building till he was hanging, then dropped to the ground. He bent over Tony, running his finger along the edge of his blade.

"Let me finish the job," he said.

"We ain't got time," pleaded Zamora.

Cunnard made a gasping sound and finally got his words out. "We're not going to do anything but burn that barn. Get those matches from my pocket, Charlie."

At this moment, there was the sound of running feet in the passageway between this building and the barn, and Dennison's booming voice. "Tony, anything happened back there yet? We've got one of them bottled up in the alley by the saloon."

Charlie wheeled in that direction, a startled, whitened expression on his brutal face. The Scorpion grabbed Cunnard's arm, pulling him toward the bank.

"My horse . . . it's in the passage there . . . we've got to get out . . . !"

Cunnard pulled back, but Charlie wheeled to catch his other arm, and between them they turned the sick man down the alley. Zamora darted to where Cunnard's gun lay and backed along with them. Dennison ran heavily into the open, puffing like a steer with too much tallow. He caught sight of them and flung himself for cover just as Zamora fired. The bullet chipped adobe from the corner of the building.

"Brick," he shouted. "Boys. They're back here . . . the whole bunch of them!"

It was almost dark now. The pound of other feet running down that passage reached the Scorpion. She and the others had made the slot by the bank. La Rubia fretted and reared as she tried to help Cunnard into the saddle.

"Get on down the alley," she told the other two men. "There's a livery in the next block. Maybe you can make it and find horses there."

Zamora and Charlie broke from cover, heading for the farther shadows of the alley. Dennison began firing from his slot. Zamora threw his arms up with a sick cry and tumbled over onto his face. Charlie darted behind a spindle fence. There was a wild squawking of chickens, and the grunt of a pig, and Charlie's vile cursing. The Scorpion threw a shot at the corner of the building, sending Dennison back into cover, and then swung the palomino out into the alley, trying to swing up behind Cunnard.

As she did this, men appeared at the street end of the passage between the bank and the office building and, with sight of her, began to fire. It spooked La Rubia. With a wild whinny, the big golden horse broke into a run. The Scorpion tried to run beside her and catch the saddle, swinging up. Cunnard was bent low over the horn, still too sick and whipped to aid her. Their direction caused the bank to block them off from those men at the street end of this slot, but Dennison began firing once more from his position farther down the alley.

The Scorpion made a last jump at the running horse. But the frightened animal was already outdistancing her. She struck the churning rump, fell off to roll across the alley, and come up against the wall of the bank. The palomino thundered on down the alley, with Cunnard rocking and swaying in the saddle. Dazed, shaken, the Scorpion got to her hands and knees and darted into the space between the bank and the next building, just as Dennison came completely into the open, reloading his gun, and other men streamed from the next passageway down.

The Scorpion ran halfway down her own narrow slot to a window. It looked in upon a darkened room. She tried to force it open, but could not. Then she deliberately broke the glass with the butt of her gun, and cleaned it out with swift, vicious swipes. She crawled through, tearing her pants, her shirt. She crouched there a moment, panting desperately. The sound of running feet and shouting voices filled her ears.

"She ducked in this alley. I heard a window breaking. Maybe she's in the doctor's office."

The Scorpion crossed this darkened room to a door, opening out into a hall. The windows of this hall, their shutters standing open, looked out upon a flagstoned patio, with the other wing of this building across that. There were poplars and willows in the patio, with branches that scraped the rooftop of the building. Remembering what Charlie had done and hearing the man closing in behind her, the Scorpion slipped over the low sill of an open window into the patio. Holstering her gun, she climbed atop a table under a tree. This brought her belly high to its lower branches, and she swung up to one, climbing from it to the next, and along this to the roof's edge. She dropped off on the earthen roof and went to her belly here, breathing heavily. The adobe wall was several feet higher than the roof level, forming a parapet that afforded a screen.

Too played out for further movement, she lay there, listening to the sounds of the search in the alley below, her body filled with the wild, breathless tension of a trapped animal.

V I

I T was late in the evening when the Scorpion finally dared move off the roof. She knew they were still searching for her, because now and then men would pass down the alley or circle into the patio, muttering in low voices. She dropped down the same way she had come up, crouching at the corner of the building and listening for sounds in the alley. After a space of silence, she passed down the alley and across the rear of the bank. She knew that George Hall's office lay beyond the Warren barn and that he would help her out of town if she could reach him.

There were guards at the rear of the barn. She crossed the alley to a line of Mexican adobes. The back yards here were cut off by spindle fences and screened by post oaks and willows. She managed to get past the barn by utilizing this cover. Then she saw that there were lights in the rear of Hall's office. She gained this building without being seen, and listened outside a moment. There were no voices. She tried the door. It opened, and she swung inside, shutting it quickly and standing with her back against it. Hall had been at a desk, bent over a pile of papers, and was straightened in surprise. There was a half-empty decanter of whisky on the desk, and his face held a sullen, flushed look.

"What's the matter, George?" The Scorpion smiled. "The tension getting too much for you?"

"You can't stay here!" he said in thick, drunken anger. "They've got everybody in town looking for you. They know you didn't get away. They've got all the horses watched, and all the roads leading out barricaded. They got Peel Forman when he tried to break through."

"That's why I came to you," she said. "I knew you'd help me escape."

He rose slowly from the chair, anger staining his gaunt face. "No," he said viciously. "You're getting out now!"

"I'll make a big noise if you try to put me out, George," she said. "They'll get here before you could do it. I might even tell them the whole setup."

The blood drained from his cheeks, leaving them a pale, parchment texture. She saw that one of the papers on his desk was a map of the Chisos Mountains, marked over with red pencil and ink. There was a red dot where the Maine house would be, and other dots in the same area. She remembered Elijah's insinuations up at the house that Hall did not really know where the water was, and she took a chance.

"Looking for the water, George?" she asked.

He half turned his head toward the map, and she did not miss the break in his expression. He turned back, trying to cover it with anger.

"No," he said. "Of course not."

She moved to the desk, a lithe, svelte figure in the flickering illumination of the oil lamp, white flesh gleaming through the tears of her shirt. "Where is it, George?" she asked, dropping her finger to one of those red dots. "Here?"

"No, listen. . . ."

"Here, George?" She moved her finger. Then she raised her eyes. "Why don't you tell me, George? Don't you really know?"

His lips compressed in tight-held anger, the tips recessing into the gaunt hollows of his cheeks. "Of course, I know," he said stiffly.

"Elijah is beginning to suspect that you don't know where the water is at all," she said. "I guess you know what he'd do if he thought you were stringing him along in this." She saw the fear varnish his eyes and heard the small, choking sound he made. "On the other hand," she pressed in, "if someone else really did know where the water was, and you helped them out of a hole, they would owe you something, wouldn't they?"

Sweat beaded his forehead as he leaned toward her. "You *did* kill Billie Dexter, then?"

Her eyes narrowed suspiciously. "You act as if you doubted that. Maybe you know something else."

"No . . . no. . . ." He shook his head desperately, wheeled to throw himself into the chair, sitting there a long space of time, staring haggardly ahead of him. Then he poured himself a stiff drink, gulped at it. "All right," he said. "I will admit I don't know where it is. When I made this deal with Elijah, I thought I could find out. Billie Dexter was working out of the office, and he'd just come back out of the Chisos with word that he had located the water. His briefcase was full of papers and figuring, and he was all for sending word to Washington immediately that there was enough water in the Chisos to supply all of Willow Valley. I tried to keep him from that, but he wouldn't be stopped. Then I offered him a part in what Elijah and I had set up. If we can force the ranchers and homesteaders out by lack of water, by rustling and raiding, we can get the land at a small fraction of its value. Then, when the water is actually found, the price of that land will boom. Billie wouldn't join us, threatened to expose me. I had sent word to Elijah to have Jesse or somebody come down here and stop Billie. Then, when I came back to my office that day and found him dead. . . ." He broke off, rising again, a desperate hope in his eyes. "You *do* have the map . . . ?"

"Not here, George. You've got to help me out of town, first."

"Not tonight," he said. "You'll have to stay here till things quiet down. I don't even think I could get you a horse now."

She moved over to seat herself on the couch, eyes drawn by an old safe squatting behind the desk. *Would his papers be in there? Would the deeds with Maine's name be there? And the checks? Perhaps even letters?* It would be part of the proof she needed to convince Tony of her innocence. It might even be enough to convict Hall and Maine in this, if connection could be established between their operations here and Billie Dexter's murder. There was a small sound outside, and she stiffened. Then she saw how rigid Hall's body had grown, the taut, desperate look to his face. When the noise was not repeated, she told him: "Maybe you'd better have another drink. This strain has been too much for you."

"Yeah," he said thickly. "Yeah."

His foot kicked the chair as he turned, almost throwing him. He fumbled at the bottle, spilling liquor. She could see he was already on his way to a drunken stupor. There was a watch chain crossing his vest, beneath his coat. *Would a man keep his keys there?* He took a deep drink, came clumsily over to her, staring down with fogged eyes.

"Why'd you kill Billie Dexter anyway? What'd you hope to gain by getting those papers?"

"Maybe I had the same idea you did," she said. "Maybe I realized what it was worth to the man who knew where the water was, and kept its location secret till drought and Cunnard's rustling and raiding had driven most of the big operators to sell out cheap." She made her voice husky. "Maybe I needed someone to work with, George."

"Sure. Why not? You 'n' me. . . ."

He leaned down, a hand on her shoulder. Apparently he meant to kiss her. But he got off balance and fell across her lap. He made a feeble effort to get up, failed. She rolled him off onto the floor. He lay there, eyes closed, a foolish grin on his face, mumbling incoherently. Tentatively she crouched beside him, touched his arm. He did not respond. She felt beneath his coat, found the vest pocket, removed the watch from that one. In the other pocket, at the other end of the chain, were the keys.

She went swiftly to the safe, tried the keys till one opened the door. Drawers. Papers. Envelopes. At last a letter from Maine to Hall. Deeds with Maine's name. A check by

Maine made out to Hall. Quit-claim deeds by home-steaders that had never been passed on to the main office at Alpine. She heard a scraping sound behind her, but thought it was just Hall, stirring. She pawed through another drawer. Then, with a premonition, she whirled.

He lay up on one elbow, drink-filmed eyes wide with surprise and rage. There was an ugly Krider Derringer in his hand.

"You cheat," he snarled drunkenly. "You damned little cheat!"

There was a creaking sound. The bellow of the shot seemed to lift the room up, rocking it violently. The Scorpion stiffened with the expectancy of jarring pain. It did not come. Then she realized what the creaking sound before the shot had been. The door was open. The shot had come from Marshal Dexter's smoking Bisley.

"Tony," she breathed in immense relief.

"Yah," he said. "Lump on the head and all."

She saw the bitterness in his face and took a hesitant step toward him. "I had to do that, Tony. Charlie was above you on the roof with a knife. He would have killed you."

"So, instead of shooting him, you tap me," he muttered. "That sounds reasonable."

"But if I had shot him, they would have known where I really stood."

"Just where do you stand?" he asked, looking down at Hall. "I heard you double-crossing him. I been staking him out for a long time now. Somebody by the name of Elijah Maine keeps an account in Alpine. But he's never been seen. Another man does all the depositing for him. I trailed that man once, after he'd made his deposit, and he brought the book right back to Hall's."

"There's proof enough in that safe to connect both Maine and Hall with what's been going on down here," she said. "But it still doesn't show who killed your brother. The oddest part is that none of them seems to know where the water is. Maine kept questioning me about it. Hall admitted he thought he had the water's whereabouts in his hands when he started this, but that Billie wouldn't play along with him, and Billie was killed before Hall found out."

"And you couldn't tell Hall, even if you did kill my brother," Tony said acidly.

Her face twisted. "Tony, you don't still think. . . ."

"What else could I think?" he asked. "You don't even ride a straight trail with your own kind. I listened outside while you got this poor fool drunk so you could get those papers and cross him up with Maine. You never had any map in the first place. Nobody has. Billie told me he didn't make any. I saw him three days before he was killed. He said he had something much more infallible than a map, that nobody else would ever discover. You killed him for nothing."

Her body drew up. "Then why did you stop Hall from killing me? You had your choice. If you really believed I killed Billie, if you hated me as much as you claim, you would have been glad to see Hall shoot."

"I . . . I. . . ." He broke off, helplessly staring down at Hall's motionless body, mouth twisting. Then he took a deep breath, shaking his head. "I'm just soft," he said. Then he jerked his gun up angrily. "But you're not talking me out of this one. I've still got that warrant for your arrest, and I'm handing it in this time with you."

"Do they hang a woman for murder in this state, Tony?"

she asked simply, looking at him wide-eyed

The blood left his face as the implication of that struck him.

She moved across the room. "Why don't you just shoot me?" she asked. "Do you think you could stand to wait, while I was in a cell? Watching them build the gallows. Watching them lead me out there and string me up. And then, after it was all over, and you had to go back behind Papago Gap anyway, and maybe found out it wasn't the Scorpion who killed your brother . . . ?"

"Cut it out," he said, savagely.

"I thought maybe you felt that way," she said.

He stood, staring down at her with smoky things stirring in his eyes. She swayed toward him till she touched him, felt a shudder go through him. She lifted one hand up to put it around his neck. The tip of the gun jammed tighter against her.

"I haven't got any keys," he said. "And you can't get my gun from me that way."

"I don't want your gun, Tony," she said, and kissed him.

She felt his body grow rigid. Then slowly the gun muzzle dropped. His arm went around her, and he was holding her so tightly she could not breathe. There was a great roaring in her head, a deep pound of pulse shaking her body. When Tony pulled his lips away from hers, they were both trembling.

"Please, Tony," she whispered huskily. "Give me this last chance. Let me go behind the Gap. Let me find out where the water is, and who killed your brother."

His lips worked faintly against his teeth. Every muscle in his face was contracted, pulling it into a wooden thing, flat and hard. He shook his head viciously, as if desperately blocking off his own feelings.

"No. I've trusted you too far already. You've crossed me up once. If I let you go again, I might as well turn in my badge."

"All right," she snapped in a sudden rage at his stubbornness. "I'm going anyway. Shoot me if you can."

She wheeled even as she spoke, darting for the door that led into the front office. She heard the hard scuffle of his boots against the floor behind her, as he jumped after her. But she tore the door open, leaping through, slamming it at him. Running into the closing portal, he threw up an arm to keep it from smashing him in the face. Then it blocked sight of him from the Scorpion. She ran across the front office, vaulting a counter. There was a chair by the front door, and she scooped it up, wheeling to throw it at Tony as he burst through the other door.

He tried to dodge, but it caught him full, twisting him around as it knocked him back against the wall. He fell to his hands and knees from there, dropping his gun and cursing in stunned pain.

The Scorpion yanked open the front door and darted onto the sidewalk. The wooden overhang above cast her into black shadow. There were men southward along the main avenue, but they did not see her at first. There were no horses in sight, and she knew that had been done deliberately, to keep her from any chance of escape. But her one desperate hope was that Tony typified all cow-country men who would ride rather than walk, even if it was only a block they had to go.

She ran across the sidewalk to the slot between buildings,

darted down this. Halfway down, she heard the front door slam open, heard Tony's boots shake the sidewalk. She came into the back alley and gave a little gasp of relief. His Appaloosa was hitched to a willow tree three buildings down. She ran toward it. The beast started whinnying excitedly and rearing up with her rushing approach.

She knocked the hitched reins free with a blow of her palm, swung them up over the tossing head, leaped aboard. She wheeled it to race northward along the alley, coming into one street, crossing it to the alley again. Another street. A man shouting. The crack of a gun. Another block of the alley. Houses petering out now. Near the north end of town. Then she reached the last house and broke into open country. From here she could see the end of the main street and men running from the shadows there to get hidden horses. Guns stabbed the darkness with cherry blasts. She turned into the trail toward Papago Gap, and they disappeared behind her. She put her spurs to the Appaloosa, praying that Tony was the kind of man who chose his horse for bottom as well as looks.

VII

DAWN found an exhausted woman and an even more exhausted horse at the entrance of Papago Gap. She did not know how far she was ahead of the posse now. She knew that once she got beyond Papago Gap, there was little chance of the men following her in. None of them knew the way to the Maine house, and her trail would soon be lost in the crust of talus and shale covering the land.

She halted at the highest point in the Gap, looking back, without sight of them. In a weary relief, she put the horse onto the down slope, into the first of those nightmare cañons with the mysterious haze of these mountains swimming out to envelope her.

It was afternoon when she reached the Maine house, turning in through the sagging gate. She halted the jaded Appaloosa in the center of the courtyard. She slid from the saddle, almost falling. The only thing that kept her from it was a pair of hands, catching her under the arms, and she turned to see Questa. There was a strange, wild gladness in his face that startled her. She had never seen an Indian show so much feeling. He kept moving his mouth and nodding his head, patting her on the arms. Then it was Cunnard, opening the door, eyes squinted against the sun, a broad grin spreading his lips as he recognized her. He whooped like a kid, running eagerly out to greet her.

"Look who's here," he laughed. "We thought you were done for. I waited around in the benches till that posse was practically wringing my tail."

"Yes," said Cora acidly from the doorway. "Look who's here."

The Scorpion glanced at her momentarily. The woman was wearing a gaudy, fringed wrapper, pulled tightly around her full body, a Spanish comb thrust indifferently into her straggling hair, a voluptuous, undeniable beauty to her, despite the sloppy, indifferent way she kept herself. But it was her eyes that held the Scorpion in that moment filled with a naked, smoldering hatred. Then Cunnard was helping the weary Scorpion into the living room, where Elijah Maine sat at a table littered with the remains of early dinner.

"Ah, our wandering beauty returnth," he lisped. "Give her the theat of honor, Jethe. Each time thee cometh, it theemth thee hath jutht thaved you from one catathtrophe or another."

"I could've taken him," pouted Cunnard like a sullen child.

Elijah's eyebrows raised. "But Charlie thaid Dexter had you up againtht the wall. One more punch would have finithhed it. When our heroine thtepth in and neatly tapth the marthal on hith handthome head."

"So he got in a couple of lucky punches," said Cunnard viciously. "I still could have taken him."

"The point ith that thee thaved you again," chuckled Elijah. "Thee hath proven herthelf. Thee ith one of uth. Even if we did fail to burn the barn, thith time, there ith alwayth another day. And how can we fail from now on, with the fabulouth *Theñorita* Thcorpion for a thaddle-mate?"

The Scorpion dropped into a chair, searching in Elijah's puffy, unhealthy face for sarcasm, but she could find no more than the usual sly sadism in his glittering eyes, his pawky grin. Something relaxed a little way down inside her. She had gotten away with it, then. At this moment she noticed Charlie, squatting on his heels against the *banca*, over by the fireplace. He was running a callused finger up and down the blade of the inevitable *belduque*, watching her steadily, searchingly, with his opaque eyes.

"Why is it you chose to give Dexter a love tap?" he asked. "When you knew I was all set to finish it for good?"

"Maybe I had doubts about your ability to do just that," she said indifferently. "You've been talking about knifing somebody ever since I came here, and you haven't touched a thing with that pig-sticker yet."

Charlie rose spasmodically. "I'll touch you. . . ."

"Shut up!" shouted Cunnard. "Sit down." Then he threw back his head to laugh. "She's right, damn you. Sit down. You haven't so much as whittled with that knife of yours in all the time I've known you. It's probably a good thing she hit Dexter when she did."

"Of courthe," murmured Elijah. "A good thing. Now tell uth how you got away, my dear."

She shrugged. "I hid on a roof till dark. They must have had an idea that a couple of us were still trapped in town, so they took all the horses off the street. They got Peel, I understand. Dexter must have gone out after Cunnard and come back into town without knowing about the horses. Before anybody could tell him, he hitched his Appaloosa to the tie rack in front of the Topaz Saloon and went in. I jumped roofs over to there and dropped down on the horse."

Maine bent forward. "They mutht have chathed you."

"I was far enough ahead of them at the Gap, so I lost them," she said.

"Good," nodded Elijah. "Cora, have Quethta fix the Thcorpion thomething to eat. Thee muth be thtarved."

The shadows were dropping their long fingers into the room by the time the food came. They talked of the raid, while she ate, and of the possibility of another one. It was dark by the time she finished eating, and Questa had lit a pair of sputtering candles to illuminate the table. Elijah had suggested that she must be very tired, and the Scorpion was just shoving back her chair, to go to her room, when the door shuddered beneath someone's pounding.

"Elijah," called Hall's voice from outside. "Let me in. . . ."

Cora cast a twisted, puzzled glance at her father, then half ran to the door, flinging it open. The Scorpion grew rigid in her chair, as George Hall almost fell in. A horse stood hipshot and jaded, almost up on the front porch, behind him. Cora half caught him, holding him up. Realizing what was coming, the Scorpion made a lunging motion to rise, pulling at her gun in the same instant.

"Thit down," purred Elijah from the head of the table. "And don't pull your weapon."

Hand on the butt of her six-gun, she twisted her head around till she could see the gun that had appeared suddenly on the table before them, a small Pepperbox with its four barrels pointed at her. She sagged back into the chair, hand falling away from her six-gun.

"I had conthidered a pothibility like thith," lisped Elijah. "Now, George, perhapth you can tell uth what happened."

Hall dropped to a chair, gripping his shoulder, a drained, whitened look to his taut face. "She's working with Tony Dexter," he said in a voice ragged with pain. "She came to my place and got me drunk so she could get the papers from the safe. I came out of it in time to see her doing that. I would have killed her, but Dexter was staked outside. He shot me. I guess they both thought I was dead. I let them believe it. I was too weak to do anything further, anyway. He thought she'd double-crossed him, too, when she hit him on the head in the alley. But she only did that to keep Charlie from killing him."

"Well," lisped Elijah. "How interethting. Thad, in a way. I had tho hoped we could number her among uth. It grievth me deeply that the raid was a failure becauthe of you," he

186

told the Scorpion. "It grievth me even more deeply to think we have to get rid of you. Before we do that, would you like to tell uth where the map thowing the location of the water ith?"

"Why should I tell you?" she inquired.

"Either you or George," said Elijah. He turned to Hall. "Are you going to tell us, George?"

"Not now, you fool," Hall told him weakly.

"Yeth," Elijah said softly. "I want one of you to tell me where the water ith. If you won't, I'll athume you don't know where it ith . . . a thing I thuthpected for thome time anyway. You firtht, George."

Hall stared at him, with a thick, cottony silence dropping into the room. His lips worked faintly against his teeth. His eyes were wide and luminous with rage and pain. "Damn you, Elijah," he said in a guttural tone.

"I thought tho," murmured Elijah. "And now you, my dear."

The Scorpion shrugged. "I can't tell you. I don't think anybody knows where it is."

"Then you don't have the map?" asked Elijah.

"How do you know there were any maps?" she asked.

He sat heavily in his chair, staring at her. "There are wayth we could make you tell," he murmured.

"No." It came savagely from Jesse Cunnard. He had been staring at the Scorpion with unbelieving eyes. But now he turned to Elijah. "You're not doing that to her."

"You fool!" hissed Cora. "Letting a little sop-and-taters blonde like that get under your skin. We've got to get rid of her. She's dangerous."

"My daughter'th right," Elijah told them. "If you're

187

thqueamith about thith, Jethe, perhapth you'd like to go outthide while we get it over with."

"No," Jesse muttered viciously. "I don't care what she's done, who she's working for. You're not doing this to her."

"Well, you are hardly in a pothithion to choothe what we do or do not do," Maine said, looking at the Pepperbox before him. "If you don't want to go, Jethe, I think we'll take care of it right now. Charlie, would you like the honorth?"

The Mexican stood up in the shadows on the farther side of the room, walking forward till his knife blade caught the candlelight.

"Yes," he said. "Decidedly."

The Scorpion could not help the sharp, upward movement that brought her to her feet. But Elijah's hand was as swift, jerking the gun up till it pointed at her.

"Don't move any farther," he said. "It will be over very quickly, my dear."

"Listen, Elijah ," Cunnard said in a guttural, shaken voice, "you can't do this."

"You won't try and thtop uth, will you, Jethe?" asked Elijah. A sadistic brutality had deepened the grooves and creases of his face, stamping it with the same voluptuous cruelty the Scorpion had seen in Cora's face. The Scorpion felt the breath block up in her, and the sweat began to form on her brow. Charlie took another step forward. At this moment, something soft and bulky hissed out of mid-air, falling across the candles. In that last instant before light was snuffed out, she turned her head up to see Questa on the balcony and that he had thrown a blanket over the candles.

In the utter darkness that fell so suddenly, she threw herself aside. Elijah's Pepperbox blazed. She heard the bullet slam into the back of the chair she had been sitting in. She tried to pull her six-gun and dart between Elijah and Cunnard. She heard Cunnard shout something incoherent as she passed him. Then she felt steel rip up her sleeve and knew that Charlie was at one side, within reach.

She twisted away from the knife, but his hand pawed blindly to catch her, fingers clutching her elbow and sliding down to her gun wrist. He twisted savagely, and she had to drop the gun with a sharp cry of pain. She kicked out with her spike heel, catching him in the knee. He shouted hoarsely, pain rendering his grip on her wrist weak in that moment, so that she could tear free. Elijah's Pepperbox blasted again, shooting at the sounds.

"Cut it out!" shouted Charlie. "You'll hit me. She's heading for the hall."

"Get to the head of the hall, Cora!" screamed Elijah. "Thtop her!"

The Scorpion heard the violent rustling of Cora's clothing as she lunged for the hall. The Scorpion veered away from this, bumping into the newel post at the base of the stairs. She found the first step with her feet and plunged upwards.

"She's going upstairs!" Cora called shrilly.

"I'll go after her!" shouted Elijah. "Charlie, go back to the rear thtepth tho thee can't get down there. George, take the outthide balcony."

"I can't move," gasped George. "I've lost too much blood for this."

"You'll looth the retht if you don't thtop her!" shouted Elijah. "Do ath I thay!"

"Elijah," roared Cunnard, "I'll get you, if you do any-

189

thing to her. I swear I'll get you."

The Scorpion was at the top of the steps now, bumping into furniture and walls in the darkness. She ran toward the opening of the second story hall, finding it at last, with the sound of Elijah, puffing up the stairs behind her. If she could only reach that outer balcony before Hall cut her off.

She ran headlong down the hall, reaching the door of her former bedroom, tearing this open. Feeble moonlight cast a wan illumination into this room from the open windows. She closed the door so it would not reveal which room she had taken, and then rushed to the window, stepping over the low sill onto the balcony. Before she could move away, George Hall appeared at the other end of the outside balcony, dragging himself up the stairs. With sight of her, he stopped, taking his supporting hand away from the rail to put it on a gun, lifting the weapon with both hands. She threw herself backward over the windowsill as he fired, the bullet going into the wall above her head. Rolling across the floor, she came to her feet and darted back toward the door. Just as she was about to fling it open, she heard Elijah's voice, high and shrill as a woman's.

"Charlie, that you?"

Charlie's voice came hollow and muffled, as if he were yet in the well of the rear stairway. "Yeah. She ain't come back down here yet."

"Thee mutht be in one of thethe upper bedroomth," shouted Elijah. "I heard Hall thooting at her when thee tried to get through a window."

There was a slamming sound, and she knew Elijah had thrown open the door of the first room. Praying he would step inside and give her that chance, she opened her own door. A pale shaft of light lay across the hall, from that first open door up there, but Elijah must have stepped inside, for he was not in the hall. At the same time, she heard George climbing the last of those rear stairs. The Scorpion closed her own door, so the light would not betray her, and began moving toward the front, hoping to get by the room Elijah was in before he came out again. At this instant, Elijah must have reached the windows and seen Hall.

"Where ith thee? Wath that you thooting at her?"

"She popped out of that bedroom farther down," answered Hall in a weak, grating voice. "She's still inside."

The Scorpion heard Elijah turn back with a curse. She launched herself into a wild run, in a last effort to get by that door. He came lunging out just as she passed, his immense, soft body crashing into her and spinning her around, carrying her clear across the hall into the wall. Stunned, she pawed for that hand holding the gun. He tried to bring it up and fire, but she caught it in both hands, lunging down to sink her teeth deeply into the puffy flesh.

With a feminine scream, Elijah dropped the weapon, turning to tear away from the pain of those teeth. It gave her the chance to dart past him, on toward the front. She heard the heavy shuffle of his feet as he lunged after her. She ran full tilt out onto the balcony, barely stopping herself at the rail. Catching this to keep herself from falling, as she changed directions, she tried to plunge toward the stairs. But the sense of his gross form, hurtling at her, made her stop this and instead throw herself flat on the floor. His boots kicked at her head, her shoulder, as he stumbled over her body. There was a great cracking sound, as Elijah's massive weight went straight into the railing. Too late he tried to pull up. The rail had given way beneath him.

His scream plunged downward into the blackness of the living room, to be cut off sharply by the sodden sound of his body striking the floor. There was a moment of painful silence. Then Charlie called from the back end of the hall. "Elijah, what happened?"

"Father," called Cora, from a rear part of the house. "Was that you?"

"Damn you, Elijah," yelled Cunnard. "I'll kill you, I swear it."

His voice was muffled, too, as if coming from toward the rear. Sickly the Scorpion gained her feet and groped her way down the stairs. She paused at the bottom, but there was no sound from the living room. It was a long enough fall to have killed Elijah.

She felt her way through the living room, with Charlie running down the upper hall, and Cora calling for her father. The front door was ajar. The Scorpion swung it open. Before she could step out, however, she caught sight of the rider coming through the sagging gate. The moonlight was still too wan for her to recognize him in that first instant. She knew that neither Dennison nor any of the townsmen could have trailed her back here, and whoever it was had arrived too late to be following either her or George Hall by sight. He must have trailed one or the other of them, then. It would take an Indian to follow sign like that. Or a man with Indian blood in him. Tony Dexter?

She flung herself inside as the tall, broad-shouldered shape of him pulled to a halt out there in the courtyard. For a moment she had the impulse to throw herself on his mercy. But she knew there would be a shoot-out whether she did that or not, as soon as the others found out he was here. And she could not afford that yet. She had to find Questa. She had to know if she was right about the Indian, before she gave herself up to Dexter.

She wheeled back through the room. Charlie had come out on the balcony above now, and heard her movement in the darkness.

"Elijah," he asked. "Is that you?"

At the same instant, someone flung the kitchen door open. Light from this room leaped through the living room in a bright yellow shaft, outlining the shape of Elijah's body on the floor and leading like a molten river to the Scorpion. Jesse Cunnard's great frame was silhouetted in the door, blond hair back lighted to form a pale, burning outline of his massive head. The Scorpion heard a long, sighing sound come out of Charlie, up above her, and she tried to leap out of the light.

At the same moment, Tony Dexter came in through the front door. Cunnard flung himself to one side, out of silhouette, his hand forming a blurred, flashing motion before he was lost in the shadows to one side of the door. Then his gun roared. Tony jumped out of the front door, and his draw must have all been one motion. His shot formed the second detonation in the room, as he fired at Cunnard's flash.

Cunnard grunted sickly, staggering forward, squeezing the trigger. But the bullet dug into the floor as he fell on his face. The two paths of light entering the room from the open doors filled the chamber with enough illumination to see now, but it had taken them all that long for their eyes to accustom themselves. Just as the Scorpion made out

Charlie's blurred figure for the first time, up there on the balcony, Charlie was bringing his knife arm back for a throw, as if he had sighted Tony. Dexter's eyes, too, had made their adjustment. As Charlie threw, the marshal flung up his gun. The knife struck the adobe wall with a heavy thump, an inch from Tony's head, with his gun going off in his hand.

The Scorpion saw Charlie straighten up on the balcony, jerking with the shot, and did not wait any more. She was so near to the hall door that it took but one leap to put her in the shadows there.

"Scorpion," shouted Tony, "hold it! I'll shoot this time."

But she did not stop. There was still something to be decided. He had not been willing to give her a chance before. She couldn't be taken in till she had found out if she was right about Questa.

She knew Cora must still be upstairs somewhere, probably in the hall behind Charlie. There was a rear door beneath the back stairway, and she let herself out this, turning toward the corrals. Running across the open compound, she flung a look up at the outer balcony. George Hall made a dark, inert heap behind the railing up there, where he had fallen, unable to keep going.

She ducked between two sheds, heading for the cedar-post corral where Questa had put her palomino before. As she did so, another figure appeared at the other end. She was about to wheel back when she saw it was the Indian. He ran to her, catching her wrist, mouth working in mute appeal. She nodded, allowing him to lead her through the corrals and into the brush. They hit a trail, running hard, and finally burst into a clearing, where he had staked her palomino and a bareback paint. She caught at him before he mounted, then went to her knees, and began to dig in the sand. He frowned, puzzled. She tried it over again, elaborating, pretending as if she were drinking. He shook his head, and she realized he must think she was asking if there was water on this very spot.

She made the signs again, then swept her arm around in a half circle. His eyes, in the moonlight, widened in a luminous, excited way. Finally she stood up and adopted the position he had assumed down at the house, head thrown back, as if listening. He nodded finally, reluctantly, and she rose, knowing he understood.

She stared intensely at him, moonlight illumining a mingling of expressions in his face. At first, there was something wooden and stubborn. Then there was a relenting, and that look of dog-like devotion filled his eyes. She knew he must be recalling her kindness to him and how she had saved his life. Finally he nodded and turned to climb aboard the paint. She swung onto the palomino and followed him on through the chaparral.

They plunged into the first cañon penetrating the mountains that backed into tiers behind the Maine house, and followed this shadowed passage till the Scorpion lost the sense of time. The scent of huisache swept against them, sweet as honey. Then it was obliterated by the acrid smell of alkali, and powdery white dust broiled up from beneath the animals' hoofs, clogging nostrils and setting the horses to snorting and coughing. At last Questa turned aside, plunging into a thicket of mesquite that grew up the rock wall. There was a crevice here, large enough to permit the passage of a horse, a great slice taken out of the mountainside, choked with brush. Agrito clawed the Scorpion's face; nopal tore her leggin's. But she forced La Rubia on after the Indian, till they finally emerged.

It was another cañon, running parallel to the one they had just left but boxed off here so that it could not go on through to the Maine house, dipping back instead in the other direction till the mountains swallowed it. Questa turned his animal up the bone-white sand bottoming this cañon for half a mile, then swung off, and adopted the position she had seen him assume—that weird, listening posture, so like a dog sensing things beyond human ken.

The Scorpion slid off and dropped to her knees. If the water was near enough for him to feel the vibration, it must be only a few feet down. She did not know how long she had dug when signs of dampness began to show. In her excitement the Scorpion had forgotten Questa was a deaf-mute and talked to him swiftly, eagerly, panting from the exertion.

"You were right. No wonder you could feel it. A couple more feet and we'll have water."

"Will you now?" Cora Maine asked in a soft, silken rage from behind them.

The Scorpion whirled to see her, standing in the sand, blouse torn to ribbons by the brush, face and hands laced with bloody scratches, her over-ripe lips in the moonlight twisted malevolently.

"How silly of us not to think of Questa," she said. "He went out with Billie that last day Billie was with us. We should have known that was the day he found the water. We should have connected the Indian with it. But who'd connect a lazy, deaf, stupid, old Indian with something worth a million dollars. I guess nobody will ever connect him with it now, will they?"

The Scorpion rose, staring at her. "You can't kill him."

"You'd be surprised what I can do," Cora told her. "For that kind of money."

The Scorpion saw the Bowie knife in her hand now. "Maybe you could kill Billie Dexter for it," she said.

"Maybe I could," Cora answered, mouth twisting vindictively.

"And it was you who tried to kill me that first night I came to the house," the Scorpion said.

"It was," Cora told her. "Now I'll finish the job. . . ."

With a cat-like sound, low and guttural in her throat, she lunged at the Scorpion. Questa flung himself before the Scorpion, but Cora slashed out, catching him deeply across the ribs. He jumped aside instinctively from the pain of it, and Cora ran in.

The Scorpion did not make the mistake of turning away or trying to dodge aside before the blow. She saw the knife flash up, lunged under it, catching the wrist in the saddle of her thumb and forefinger as it descended, blocking the blow. Then she hooked a boot around behind Cora, lunging her weight in against the woman. They went down, clawing, biting, scratching, Cora trying to tear her wrist free, rolling back and forth in the sand. All the sadistic cruelty of her father was reflected in her determination. The Scorpion was completely on the defensive, forced to hold onto that knife wrist with all her strength, battered this way and that by the twisting fingers of the other woman.

Finally Cora got a leverage with her leg and forced the Scorpion off her with a violent turn. It rocked the Scorpion's head backward onto one of those smooth, round stones littering the river bottom. Stunned, she felt the will flee her body. With animal vindication, Cora rose to her knees above the helpless Scorpion.

In that instant, a bony brown shape crashed against Cora, knocking her aside, to roll off in the sand, hands clawing at her throat. With a scream, Cora plunged the knife into Questa. He rolled over to pin it between them, still throttling her. She made a violent effort to get the knife out, but he kept it pinched there. Her struggles ceased to be directed toward the knife, and she kicked and clawed insanely, trying to free those hands from her throat. They were like a vise that would not move. Her struggles grew weaker, ceased. For a space only Questa's hoarse breathing was audible. Then that stopped, and he sagged across the woman's body, fingers still buried in her throat.

The Scorpion rose shakily to see Tony Dexter, sitting his horse in the middle of the ancient riverbed, gun in his hand. He shrugged, put it away, swung off the animal.

"Thought I'd get a chance to use it," he said. "The Indian took care of things too quick." He stood looking for a long moment at the Scorpion. "I overheard most of your little conversation with this woman. Especially the part about her killing my brother." He gazed at her for a long time. "I'm sorry," he said at last.

She knew what he meant and answered as simply. "I don't blame you for thinking I killed your brother, Tony. I'm just glad it's over now." She gazed sadly at the Indian. "I guess that's what Billie meant when he told you he had something even more infallible than the map. Your brother apparently used Questa as a guide, and was kind to the

Indian. Maybe Questa already knew where the water was, or maybe Billie and he found it together. I don't know."

"Why do you make a point of Billie's kindness?"

"Because that was apparently why Questa helped me. I think he hated the Maines. They treated him like a dog. Both of them were capable of infinite cruelty. That's why he didn't show them the water. I guess he would have left if he were younger. A man his age wouldn't have lasted long in this country. Then I had a chance to save him from Cora. I think she was in rage enough to have killed him that day. Cunnard said it made Questa my slave for life. I guess . . . I guess he was right."

Her voice broke, and she turned her face in against Dexter, unable to look in Questa's direction any longer, wanting to get away from this now.

Dexter's arms were about her, strong and comforting. "We'll have to pick up Hall," he said. "I think he's still alive. Then we'll get out of here." He hesitated, then said: "Scorpion . . . that kiss . . . in Hall's office. Was it all just so I'd let you go?"

"It started out to be merely an expedient," she said. "I guess it was more than that before we were through."

"What did it mean . . . to you?"

"It meant you attract me, I guess," she answered. "More than any man I've met in a long time."

"No more than that?" His tone was intensely sober.

She threw her head back, something wild in her eyes. "A thing like that takes a while, Tony. I've only known you for such a short time."

"Then we'll give it time," he said, grinning suddenly. "We'll give it all my life, if it takes that."

Hearing his voice, she could tell how much he meant it. She took his hand, a promise in her face that he probably couldn't see, and then turned to lead him back to the horse.

THE END

Center Point Publishing
600 Brooks Road ● PO Box 1
Thorndike ME 04986-0001 USA

(207) 568-3717

**US & Canada:
1 800 929-9108**